SEMBENE OUSMANE was born in Senegal in 1923. Essentially self educated, he became a fisherman just like his father: 'I have earned my living since I was 15,' Sembene says. He moved to Dakar until the outbreak of World War Two, when he was drafted into the French army and saw action in Italy and Germany. Returning to Senegal for a short time, Sembene realized that in order to further his literary ambitions he would have to move to France. He went to Marseilles where he worked as a docker, joined the French Communist Party, and became a union organizer. He also began writing.

His output has been prodigious. *Le Docker noir* appeared in 1956, a semi-autobiographical novel written in Marseilles; followed a year later by *Oh Pays, mon beau peuple!* about the problems of re-adaptation encountered by an African returning home with a French wife and new ideas. Three years later, *Les Bouts de Bois de Dieu* was published. In 1962 Ousmane wrote *Voltaïque*, a volume of short stories which included the story *La Noire de . . .* which he later turned into a prize winning film. A fourth novel, *L'Harmattan*, was released in 1964, after which Ousmane had the opportunity to study at the Moscow film school. Two more short novels – *Véhi Ciosane ou Blanche Genèse (White Genesis)*, and *Le Mandat (The Money-Order)* – followed, the latter becoming a film that won a prize at the Venice film festival and established Ousmane's reputation as a director. In 1973 another novel, *Xala*, was published, going on to become one of a series of successful films. Ousmane's latest novel appeared in 1981 – the massive two volumed work *Le Dernier de l'empire*.

Heinemann publish several of Ousmane's novels in translation: *Les Bouts de Bois de Dieu* as *God's Bits of Wood*, *Le Mandat suivi de Véhi Ciosane* as *The Money-Order with White Genesis*, and *Xala. Le Docker noir* appeared in Autumn 1987, as *Black Docker*.

SEMBENE OUSMANE

THE MONEY-ORDER
WITH WHITE GENESIS
TRANSLATED BY CLIVE WAKE

HEINEMANN

Heinemann International
a division of Heinemann Educational Books Ltd
Halley Court, Jordan Hill, Oxford OX2 8EJ

Heinemann Educational Books (Nigeria) Ltd
PMB 5205, Ibadan
Heinemann Kenya Ltd
Kijabe Street, PO Box 45314, Nairobi
Heinemann Educational Boleswa
PO Box 10103, Village Post Office, Gaborone, Botswana
Heinemann Educational Books Inc.
70 Court Street, Portsmouth, New Hampshire, 03801, USA
Heinemann Educational Books (Caribbean) Ltd
175 Mountain View Avenue, Kingston 6, Jamaica

LONDON   EDINBURGH   MELBOURNE
SYDNEY   AUCKLAND   SINGAPORE
MADRID   HARARE

British Library Cataloguing in Publication Data

Ousmane, Sembene
The money order; with, White genesis.–
(African writers series).
I. Title   II. Vehi ciosane ou Blanche-genèse,
suivi du Mandat. *English*   III. Series
843[F]   PQ3987.0/

ISBN 0-435-90894-4
ISBN 0-435-90895-2 Export

Printed in Great Britain by
Richard Clay Ltd, Bungay, Suffolk

CONTENTS

VEHI-CIOSANE
or
WHITE GENESIS

2

———————

He was one of the companions of my youth.
Together we underwent the ordeal of initiation.
He believed in the God of *Gain*, in happiness
through *Money*. After the '39-'45 war, he enlisted
in the French Expeditionary Corps.

He died penniless in Indochina, in June '54.

My old friend Boca Mbar
Sarr PATHÈ

LIFELESS

PATHÈ

Is it on the top of the hill
Is it between two paddy fields
Is it on the edge of the woods
Is it in the water that carried you off
Is it on the path

   Nowhere the mound
   Of your grave

   Not even a heap of rubbish
   A strip of ground
   The remains of a body
   A piece of stem

To plant
On your dead death
A grave a foot long
Without an epitaph
You lie there beneath this mound

Above the wind blows
The rain washes away the soil
Melancholy shapes wander about
The men and women of this country
Still struggle ...
... Not any more against France

It is America 'the light of the free world'
that bombards your grave twenty years after ...
A dead death for nothing

    The cross has gone
    The earth has gone
    Where is your grave

    It was a small life
    An epithet in wood.

PATHÈ

Ah! ... old companion
Born in the same village
No wife to shed a tear
No fiancée no mother no child
Not even a grave

    Poor mother Africa
    Sterile you might have been a paradise
    for your sons ...

—————————

Sometimes, into the most ordinary low caste family, a child is born who grows up and glorifies his name, the name of his father, of his mother, of his whole family, of his community, of his tribe; even more, by his work he ennobles MAN.

More often, in a so-called high caste family which glories in its past, a child comes into the world who, by his actions, sullies his entire heritage, does harm to the honest MAN he encounters and even robs the individual diambur-diambur of his dignity.

———————

THE STORY I AM GOING TO TELL YOU TODAY IS AS OLD AS the world itself. The most primitive institutions, as well as the relatively more complex institutions of our own time, are inflexible in their condemnation of the crime which is its subject. In some countries, though, it is only a crime when the girl (or boy) is a minor. But, of course, there is still the moral aspect of the question.

Over the years, I have often discussed it with you, my fellow AFRICANS. Your reasoning has never convinced me. However, on one point you were agreed: I must not write this story. You argued that it would bring dishonour to US, THE BLACK RACE. Worse still, you insisted, the detractors of the NEGRO-AFRICAN CIVILIZATION would latch onto it and ... and ... and ... use it to cover us with shame.

To avoid appearing pedantic, I will not analyse your attitudes to this problem. But when will we stop acknowledging and approving our actions in terms of the other man's colour, instead of in terms of our HUMANITY? Racial solidarity certainly exists, but it is subjective and it has not prevented the reigning dynasties of modern black Africa from committing murder, detaining people without trial and gaoling others for political motives.

I also know, and so do you, that in the past, as well as in the present, there have been many anonymous heroic actions among us. But not everything we have done has been heroic. Sometimes, therefore, in order to understand a period fully, it is good to concentrate our minds on certain things, on certain deeds, and certain kinds of action. For they enable us to descend inside MAN and his failure, and to assess the extent of the damage.

The debility of AFRICAN MAN—which we call our AFRICAN-ITY, our NEGRITUDE, and which, instead of fostering the subjection of nature by science, upholds oppression and engenders venality, nepotism, intrigue and all those weaknesses with which we try to conceal the base instincts of man (may at least one of us shout it out before he dies)—is the great defect of our time. The exaggerations of intellectual speculation are brought to bear upon our contemporary society, our link with the past and the future, and upon the sense of community of our fathers and our great-grandfathers. These intellectual prima-donnas know nothing (or pretend to know nothing) about our fathers' and our grand-fathers' times, when the SAHHE (granary) was our pride. They know nothing about the needs of the men of those times and their passive, sometimes active, resistance to the occupier. They know nothing about the disintegration of community.

I cannot myself say how this story began. It is always pretentious—or so it seems to me—to think that one can unravel the origins of a drama of this kind.

I know that you exist, VEHI. Perhaps when you are old enough to go to school, you will find a place and later you will read these lines. More probably, like thousands of others of your generation, you will never read them. The present symptoms of our society do not permit me to predict a better life for you. When you reach the age of awareness, you will rebel, like thousands of others as anonymous as you, but, whether it is individual or collective, it will be a futile revolt because it will be badly directed.

Your mother, our contemporary, illiterate in French as well as Arabic, will have no chance to read these pages. She lives alone; it is a way of clothing herself in her drama.

As for you, VEHI-CIOSANE NGONE WAR THIANDUM , may you prepare the genesis of our new world. For out of the defects of an old, condemned world will be born the new world that has been so long awaited and for so long part of our dreams.

Ndakaru, Gamu 1965.

THE NIAYE IS IN THE SINGULAR IN WOLOF. THE COLONIAL-
ISTS wrote it in the plural. It is neither savannah, nor delta, nor
steppe, neither bush nor forest. It is a very strange zone bordering
the Atlantic Ocean in the west and stretching from Yoff to Ndar,
and beyond. Villages and clusters of dwellings sprang up from it,
as ephemeral as drops of water on the eyelashes. It begins at
Pikine, the famous battleground recalled from time to time
by the griots: a vast expanse without end, its soft hills clad,
according to the season, with every variety of vegetation: short,
bottle-green grass, growing in one season only, the navet, the rainy
season; massive dwarf baobabs with their delicious fruit (the leaves
of the baobab, known as lalo, are dried, pounded and strained,
and used to season couscous, giving this dish its flavour and making
it light to the palate); oases of coconut trees; tall palm trees
growing at random, with long, clumsily plaited, waving leaves;
rhun palms, gaunt and rough of aspect, defying the sky with their
tall trunks and fan-shaped crests of leaves, measuring themselves,
first against the dawn, then against the sunset; groves of mahogany
trees dense with leaves, their branches falling to the ground
like Fula huts and inhabited by cruel ants. Nere, kada and other
trees whose names I do not know spread their branches, providing
generous shade according to the season, and a resting place for
the minute birds of the niaye when they are exhausted.

Pools of stagnant water, covered with the dark green leaves of
water-lilies, are surrounded on their banks by a lacework of
small palm trees whose sap oozes plentifully, giving off a delicious,
intoxicating scent. Pools do not have the same kind of vegetation
as lakes.

As he makes his way across the niaye, the stranger's gaze is
held by the impression of a retreating horizon, or by the feeling
that he has made no progress: uniformity ... clumps of cactus,
prickly pears, vradj and sump merge with one another and break
up the undulating, creamy white monotony of the sand. On
the horizon, receding, obstinate, irregular, line upon line of dunes.
Above, the sky, the continentally vast African sky, like liquid
mercury, depending on the month.

By midday, overcome, beasts and insects seek cover. The whitish vapour, like a hot bath, begins to rise, creating the illusion of a moving sea. A veil of light blue indigo blends with the curving, broken line of the infinite.

The grass of the previous navet sinks, dead and broken, into the soft sand. The sumps bristle with thorns, like harrows. The dead leaves that have not been able to take root are all swept up by the wind and caught, fluttering, in the thorns. Except during the navet, a long whistling sound, on a single note, can be heard coming from all over the niaye. At dusk, this whistling becomes lugubrious. Our grandparents used to say the niaye was whimpering.

The torrid atmosphere immobilizes the entire animal world. The beetles and the big black and grey poisonous spiders bury themselves under their beds of dry leaves. Lizards, snakes and reptiles of every variety coil themselves up. There is no sound of life from the insects and birds, except when the occasional crow or sparrow-hawk, driven from its shelter by another stronger than itself, wheels above the niaye, wailing the wail of the weak.

All this is enclosed inside the immense, silent loneliness of the niaye: the enforced retreat of the middle of the day.

As the sun sinks, the hills, the palm trees, the kadas, sumps, baobabs, coconut trees, mahogany trees and rhun palms are all released from its oppressive tyranny. Their silhouettes lengthen, and they project their shadow onto the ground, turned to the colour of rancid butter. The animal life, freed from its confinement, returns to its rough existence, tracing a complex filigree on the sand. The niaye keeps pace with the setting sun, second by second unfolding the spectacle of its many shades. Far off, in the direction of the sunset, flimsy layers of clouds, ranging from bright saffron to the turquoise blue of a boubou just drawn from the dye, relay one another, for the delight of the eye. During the navet, when the young grass covers the ground in a uniform shade of garish green, the niaye and its sunsets are still one of those sights one returns to over and over again.

As the sun sets, the sharp distinction of objects and plants and the humps of the dunes come together and merge into one.

At night, it is impossible to measure the niaye with the eye: it is a waterless depth. Above, an immense sky pierced by countless white tips. The inhabitants of the niaye, in admiration, say: 'The mountain is no higher than the sand dune. At most, it is only a mound made up of more grains of sand.' Others reply: 'Certainly, this is true. But, to be logical, an ant on top of the mountain is higher than the mountain.'

However far you 'descend' into our past, as far back as our grandfathers (not forgetting the three centuries of the slave-trade and one century of colonialism), there have never been any stone or brick houses in the niaye. Nothing that would make it possible for strangers to say: 'Here lived resourceful men and women who were concerned about their own time, but who also thought about the future and the passing of time.' No arched doorways, no stone houses surrounded by raised verandas, no gardens with flowers arranged in patterns according to their colours, no monuments to the glory of the first men, no sepulchres to give witness to the past.

Santhiu-Niaye, where the events of our story take place, was no different from other villages. It did not attract the thousands of Senegalese who, each year, made their way, if they were Muslims, to Tiwawan, Touba or Ndiassane, or, if they were Christians, to Popenkine. Its inhabitants were never visited by the Black Virgin, nor by a sheikh, and none of them ever had the good fortune to go to the Kaaba or to Rome.

Yet they were true believers, wearing away the skin of their foreheads and their knees in prayer: five times a day. There was neither school nor dispensary, and what would have been the point of a police-station? The authorities came once a year to collect the taxes, and one year was much like another.

Before our drama (if such it was) began, Santhiu-Niaye had seen its star shine and its pulse had beaten with the vitality of our fathers' and our grandfathers' day, when the sahhe was the symbol of provision for the future. Each family had its field in which it grew maize, millet, groundnuts, cassava and sweet potatoes. In the shadow of the main hut, the sahhe, the pride of the family, attracted attention according to its size.

Now, in our time, year by year, like a natural disaster, the able-bodied men went to seek their fortune in the towns where, it seemed, life was easier. Navet after navet, the crops became poorer and poorer. The heads of families, their faces scorched by too much sun, their strength spent in vain, turned in on their instinct of self-preservation with an unconscious virulence: they had a foreboding of a future which even now filled them with terror. They sought comfort in the adda, the tradition, and in the hypo-thetical promise of one of the best places in paradise. Allah's paradise, like a nail fixed in the centre of their brain, the corner-stone of every activity of their daily existence, weakened and breached their faith in the future. Burying themselves in the old saying: 'Life is nothing', they had reached a state where they no longer felt desire. At the limits of their life here below nothing stood out, nothing which could rouse the covetousness of desire. Once the need to exist (and not to live) had been satisfied, the rest—and what was the rest, anyway?—was futile. But beyond the rest was human self-respect.

The impoverishment around them—that total impoverishment that blinds the spirit—made them incapable of sacrificing them-selves for their children, or of thinking it possible they might do so. That burning desire for self-sacrifice, the gift of self for others, the refusal to give in, the rejection of the atavistic instinct, which is the first step towards the future, was for these people a betrayal of their faith, an act of defiance and a moral crime against the ancient established order.

And Santhiu-Niaye, emptied of its will to act, became depopula-ted, stagnated. Between the gaps in the collapsing fences, in the peinthiu, the village square, beneath the tree where the old men came to sit and watch the time pass, life seeped away, mono-tonously. The drums were no longer heard on moonlit nights. And worse still, at the turn of the night, when the great sleepy log covers with its head of ashes the embers that tomorrow morning will be used to relight the fire in the hearth, you no longer heard the triumphant whistling of the young lover as he returned with happy tread from the hut of his beloved. The gaze of the young girls was cold. Their doe's eyes, usually alert for every gesture, every word, no longer looked into the eyes of the young men for whom their hearts beat. They composed no songs, or perhaps they had forgotten how to. They sang the songs their mothers had composed when they were young girls. These songs their mothers had sung long ago were full of life. They had composed them during their nocturnal tussles, or in the ardour of competition as they worked in the fields, reaping maize, millet and groundnuts. Now, these songs recalled the happy times that were past, intensifying their mothers' sadness and the unhappiness they felt in the absence of suitors for their daughters. The mothers: '*I salute you, women, here and everywhere. Deep as the sea! You are the earth. So deep, so wide is the sea, you are the sky above, the sea-bed beneath and the other bank.*' With aching and heavy heart, they listened to the songs they had composed long ago. Dominated by their men, fearful of today's realities and sick at heart, the mothers said nothing.

The season's cycle followed its course. The strange character of the niaye bound the people together, yet kept them apart.

Seen from the top of the sand dune, the huts of Santhiu-Niaye stood in rows according to a law of planning peculiar to the people of those parts: in rows according to family and rank. The houses lay like a young girl, shivering and frightened in her nakedness, her hands clasped between her thighs.

———

THE DOG LET OUT ITS HOWL AGAIN, FOLLOWED BY THE same yapping. Ngone War Thiandum woke with a start from her refreshing sleep. All the prejudices against this animal of hell and all the baleful tales told about it passed through her mind.

The hut was in the deepest darkness. In the sleeping village, only the howl of the dog was alive. Ngone War Thiandum listened intently for some distant sound. But she could hear nothing.

Neither yesterday, nor the day before, nor even the day before that, had she gone further than the door of the kitchen, even though these were the three days of her aiye, when it was her turn to be with her husband. She leant back against the bamboo partition. All at once her real obsession flooded into her mind. The strong, regular breathing of her husband filled the hut. Over the years—more than twenty-five—Ngone War Thiandum had become used to this breathing, to this body, to this arm that touched her now with its fingers. In the darkness of the hut, like water blackened by the ink of a squid, she could make out her husband's mouth, not too large, with strong teeth; his ears, loose like all the Ndiobene, the Diob family; his round head, with its near-white hair, which he shaved off once a month.

The mattress rustled. Was the shape coming to life? No ... The fingers withdrew from their haven of sleep. A foot, warm, asleep, anchored itself to her feet. Her heart missed a beat. The rushing of her blood barely kindled the half-memories that stumbled on the reefs of her past. She tried to forget this past, to forget this body, but she could not, even by doing violence to her memories. Just as clods of earth, like sponge, blend together, grain by grain, so her memories met and intermingled with one another. A lull would give her brief respite, and sleep would embrace her, only to be broken, suddenly, and plunge her once again into a state of agitation. She could do nothing to calm the surging of her breast. Her mind hovered between one crest and another of her past life and her present. Then she would take up the thread of a new, horrible existence, and the realization that all her past life, fed on fine precepts, had been nothing but lies. She had merely been the prisoner of a morally false order. 'If not, why this act, and how?' she asked herself.

The body gave out a loud rattle. From her foot there came an unpleasant sensation. Because of his foot on her shin, everything in her was sensitive at this point of contact. She was unable to detach her thoughts from that spot. The disgust her body felt for this limb deprived her of any kind of aggressive movement, and held it, like a canoe stranded on the mud of the Casamance, waiting to rot.

Ngone War Thiandum had had enough of this persistent misery. The nervous curiosity that had driven her to find out, in dribs and drabs, the identity of the father of the illegitimate child her daughter was carrying, had suddenly left her. Again she listened for the signs that a new day was dawning. Struggling against the grip in which she was held by her inertia, she felt the desire to rebel for once, for just once in more than twenty years, and withdraw her foot. She gave in, morally defeated. She hated herself in her defeat and was filled with a deep contempt for her life. As she had made her way through life, the life of her family (the Thiandum-Thiandum, of whom she was, now, the only survivor), she had been careful to do so without departing from the course her predecessors had laid down for her and bequeathed her, embroidering it with their names and their blameless conduct. She had been united to the Ndiobene, a clan as noble as hers, and whose names were as legendary as those of her family. But now their guelewar, noble lineage had been tainted by an incestuous act, bringing dishonour greater than any insult on the Ndiobene and the Thiandum-Thiandum.

The words of the sage came, luminous, into her mind: 'Sometimes a child is born into the most ordinary low caste family who grows up and glorifies his name, the name of his father, of his mother, of his whole family, of his community, of his tribe. More often, in a so-called high caste family which glories in its past, a child comes into the world who, by his actions, sullies his entire heritage, and even robs the individual diambur-diambur of his dignity.' She repeated these words to herself, but still she hesitated to act.

The rest of the night was long, longer than the preceding nights. It was the last night of her aiye (according to the immutable law of polygamy, until sunrise everything there was hers, man and objects). She plucked up courage to withdraw her foot carefully, got out of bed, and closed the door behind her.

Outside, a few stars still shone, the last for that night.

'Yallah, have pity on me, a simple woman! Drive from me dark, stubborn thoughts of vengeance. My Yallah, I have always obeyed your commandments, and interpreted what I have heard. You have been my guide and my witness, your malaika, your angels, have been my close companions. When I was a young girl, like all young girls, I looked into the eyes of the people who were my age, laughed, ran and danced with frenzy upon the earth. When I was in great haste, I scalded the ground, the ground that was swollen with the presence of the dead, with the dead of others. Was that a sin? I beg you to forgive me, Yallah. When I became a woman, I ceased to be a woman: my heart smiled no more at other men, my mind was given no more to carnal thoughts. I was humble, my Yallah, as you wish it, as you desire it for your subjects. I remained a wife and a mother without complaining, without blaming the infidelities of my husband. I was submissive to my lord, my master after you, Yallah, my guide in this world, my advocate in the next, according to your teaching. I only rested when my lord rested. My voice never rose above his. In his presence, I always kept my eyes on the ground. Astafourlah! Perhaps not every day, Yallah. I have always obeyed him, knowing that I was obeying your will. Yallah! Forgive me! But why this act? Why?'

The neck of the bottle from which these thoughts poured was suddenly blocked. Ngone War Thiandum could not tell whether it was a prayer or an accusation she was addressing to Yallah, or whether in some roundabout way she was judging her life and the rule of her life. Exhausted, she rested after her mental effort. The weight of so many days and nights clouded the horizon of her peace of mind. Deep down, she longed for Santhiu-Niaye to disappear. On the screen of her mind, she watched with satisfaction the concessions and their inhabitants being swallowed up, one by one, by the dunes. She rejected the community that had turned its back on her and left her alone with her shame.

Like all the women of these parts, Ngone War Thiandum had her place in society, a society sustained by maxims, wise sayings and recommendations of passive docility: woman this, woman that, fidelity, unlimited devotion and total submission of body and soul to the husband who was her master after Yallah, so that he might intercede in her favour for a place in paradise. The woman found herself a listener. Outside her domestic tasks she was never given the opportunity to express her point of view, to state her opinion. She had to listen and carry out what her husband said. Ngone War Thiandum had come to believe that what a man said had more sense in it than her own tortuous ideas. She was a woman and, of all women, she thought, she had never had an intelligent idea. When she had become a mother, she had ordered her own life and the lives of her children according to received moral principles. Now, an abominable act had transfixed itself between this degrading present and a past worthy of honour. She struggled with herself to recover the numbing happiness of the moral existence she had known before. A powerful force within her drained her and drew her towards the threshold of the drama that was undermining her and destroying her dignity. She resisted fiercely, spurred on by a burning desire to be free.

In the end, this self-doubt gained a hold on her, finding that healthy life a fertile soil in which to take root. Her life which, until now, had been sustained by the laws of the Koran and the adda, surrendered. Tormented, her will broken, she was an easy prey to predispositions deriving in part from the passions, and today's act forced her to question the precepts which, until yesterday, had been the obvious basis of her life. Like a tear, a tiny hole which she unconsciously enlarged, she fell in with her realization—a new step for her—that she could judge events from her own, woman's point of view. This new responsibility was a shattering experience for a woman like herself, whose opinions had always been decided for her by someone else.

She went into her hut, only to come out again almost immediately. The cocks were calling to one another from every compound. Then rose the node, the muezzin's call, scattering itself in all directions. In spite of her great mental pain, Ngone War Thiandum had her bath and performed the first prayer of the morning. She then went and hid herself behind the small bamboo screen which separated her from the rest of the dwelling. There she said her beads, alone.

Santhiu-Niaye was waking up. The thudding of pestles grew louder. Like an eye lazily opening its lashes, the sun gazed down on the niaye.

Ngone War Thiandum was far away, remote. None of the morning sounds around her woke the least glimmer of interest in her. The echo of the thudding pestles resounding through the village, the pots that had been forgotten the night before in the yard, the cracked calebashes waiting to be repaired, a log being salvaged from a burnt-out fire, twigs being collected to make brooms, the fear that the embers of a fire might be scorching the ground and the dead buried in it, all these daily activities, all of them elements of her life as a woman and a wife, left her indifferent.

Everyone noticed this detachment from all the things that bound her to others. Afraid that what she knew might be divulged, she hid her gaze. She lowered her eyes, and did not look directly at people or things. The unhappy feeling that she was an object of contempt made every part of her body cry out, even her lips which no longer inspired her with confidence. Was it not true that her lips could speak independently of her will? She was afraid of them, so kept her head down to hide them. Her dread of being betrayed or ostracized forced her in on herself. She was haunted by the anxiety born of the horror of being a laughing-stock, of being the village cesspit, she who sprang from a family that had been guelewars from father to son and had never known the least slur. To think that, behind her back, people would say:

'Don't you know?'

'No. Tell me.'

'It's simple. What everyone thought isn't true. It's not a stranger who got her daughter pregnant.'

'What do you mean?'

'It's as true as the day.'

'Who was it then?'

'Who? Do you really need to ask?'

'By my ancestors, I don't know.'

'Come closer. There! ... Just make sure no one's about. There!

... It was her husband, the father of her daughter, Guibril Guedj Diob.'

'Astafourlah! Astafourlah! Eiye! Eiye! What are you saying?'

'It's as true as the day.'

'Is it possible? Spend the day in peace! No need to tell me the details.'

Behind the mbagne-gathie, the bamboo screen that preserves one's privacy, she heard the voice of her third veudieu (co-wife). She was chiding the children. For a moment, her mind attached itself to the co-wife's words.

Ngone War Thiandum found it difficult to return to her state of communion with Yallah. She held her beads in her hand, her brain torn violently apart like the crater of an emptying volcano. She whimpered, like a frustrated lioness. When the storm within her died down and calm momentarily returned, her feeling of apathy would rise to the surface and the image of her daughter, Khar Madiagua Diob, would play like filigree on the reflections of her imagination. She saw her as a coquette, indulging in coquetry of the most elementary kind. She could hear the happy band of young girls squabbling about the children they would have and how they would run their homes. They would argue hotly about marriage and the advantages and disadvantages of being the first wife, saying that she aged much sooner than the second, third or fourth wife. Ngone War Thiandum, having lived through all the phases of marriage, was full of advice and pointed out the disadvantages of being second wife, thinking all the time of the man who would be her son-in-law. She wanted and prayed that her daughter, Khar Madiagua Diob, might have a hard-working, pious man for a husband, a man of good caste and spotless lineage.

Since the pregnancy of her daughter, these dreams had been scattered like pieces of straw caught up in a whirlwind, and lechery had reared its head like some insidious perfume. Agitated, she pressed the bead between her finger and thumb; her jaws shut tight, her teeth clenched, so violent was the suffering that wracked her. The desire to hurt someone, to make her husband and her daughter—or, failing them, someone else—suffer, but not to kill them, nearly deprived her of her self-control. But she strangled the cry that rose from her belly, a cry she had suppressed so long; it tore itself from her throat, taking with it pieces of burning flesh. She struggled to keep a grip on herself, and her cry came out in a gasp, with a shudder of desperate supplication. It was the cathartic explosion of undirected thought. Her whole body was on fire.

She did not see Gnagna Guisse arrive, until her shadow fell on her. She lifted her ravaged face, her eyelids puffed by three sleepless nights. Her gaze took in Gnagna Guisse from head to foot. Gnagna Guisse looked at her and caught the dancing glimmer of fear on her face—that face she had known to be sober and without guile—and, at the corners of her mouth, the shadow of bitterness. Gnagna Guisse was the same age as she was, just past forty, and belonged to the griot caste: she was her gueweloi-diudu, her genealogical griot. An old friendship bound them in a rather special way, as friendship usually does among women in our part of the world. They were inseparable and always went to the well together. If one was late, the other preferred to wait. The same cake of henna served them both, the same calebash of antimony, which they used to brighten their lashes and eyebrows and their tattooed lower lip. The one never returned from a visit to the town without a gift for the other, unless she came back with nothing for herself either. They were not content with sharing the same tastes. They wanted to be alike in everything, in their dress and in the way they plaited their hair. After they were married, their roles as wife and mother, and the accidents of birth, obliged them to go their separate ways, but their youthful friendship never lost any of its warmth.

Ngone War Thiandum moved up, inviting her friend by this gesture to sit beside her on the tree-trunk. Ngone War Thiandum did not linger over the exchange of banal morning greetings. She replied briefly, using the formal phrases. She waited anxiously to hear what the griot would say. And, as she waited, she became impatient, and the painful emotion over which she had been brooding for months swelled like the tide, overtook and overwhelmed her.

Gnagna Guisse, an expert, thanks to her experience as a griot, in gauging a woman's feelings, took in the situation at a glance. Watching her out of the corner of her eye, she saw how the sinews of her neck stood out and relaxed, in spasms. Aware of her role, she acted as if she knew nothing and, circumspectly, she said:

'Ngone, Ngone, my friend, everyone is worried about you. You avoid our company. Has someone done something to you?'

'No, no one has insulted me,' she answered, suppressing the reply that was on the tip of her tongue.

'What's wrong, then? For months you have been pining and brooding. I can understand the suffering you feel as a mother, and your disappointment, but what can you do now? No one can escape his destiny. If it is true, as it is written, that our every act is recorded before we are born, that we are only unfortunate actors in this life, then you ought to put your confidence in Yallah. Yallah sees everything, knows everything. He alone is judge. Only he is qualified to judge each of us.'

Ngone War Thiandum bowed her head. 'Does she know something?' she wondered. 'How has she managed to deduce my secret?' Aloud:

'If it is true that everything is decided by Yallah, why is there a moral law? Why exalt good and condemn evil? Do these principles have any purpose? In any case, I don't really know what you mean.'

Having managed to control her voice sufficiently to say this, Ngone War Thiandum raised her head. The smile she forced her face to shape was betrayed by the obvious rigidity of her features, and on her eyelids hung her weariness and her obstinacy. Gnagna Guisse returned the mother's gaze; her eyes were held prisoner by her look. In her turn, the griot withheld the harsh reply she had already gathered in her throat. She said:

'I am talking about Khar's condition. Do you think it is right that she should have to carry this cross at her age? No! It is also true that no mother likes it, nor would she like it. But the fact is there.'

'And I must get on with it?' Ngone War Thiandum interrupted. After a pause: 'What are people saying in the village?'

'There is a little talk. Of course, tongues are wagging, and enjoying it, and people are still wondering who the father is. But it will pass and be forgotten. But you are eating your heart out about it.'

'Gnagna,' interrupted the mother, the sinews in her neck standing out more than ever. 'Gnagna, that isn't all they are saying. Stop deceiving me ...'

'I lie to you? Me?'

'No, of course not. That isn't what I meant.'

'What, then?'

Ngone War Thiandum was possessed by a mixture of despair and rage which, as she spoke, seemed to make her heart leap from her breast. 'I'm all on fire,' she said to herself. 'I'm all on fire.' She didn't want to be put off any longer. She went on:

'People observe, they comment and they gossip. Look at Tanor (her eldest son, who had fought in Indochina and North Africa), the children make fun of him because he is mad. In a way, it is better for him, now. He doesn't suffer. Morally, I mean. Yet he was the finest young man of his generation. You remember him, when he returned from his military service. It was you who welcomed him, spreading fine cloths beneath his feet.'

'I remember.'

'I expected to see a man. It was less than a man I welcomed home. I was proud when he went away, and anxious, too. He came back to me insane. One does not show courage by invading others, but by facing indignity in one's own country. A curse on war and rank! War deprives me of a son to wash away my dishonour, and my sense of rank wracks me.'

'Don't forget, I am your griot. Stop eating your heart out. Your husband will take care of things. Men don't take women into their confidence; they act, and present us with the accomplished fact.'

'That is true enough. This morning I finished my aiye.'

'I understand,' said Gnagna Guisse.

'You understand nothing. Nothing at all,' the mother exploded. There was a pause.

The muscles of her face were tense. Her forehead wrinkled as incomprehension and her inner struggle asserted their hold on her. At the same time, her tattooed lower lip curled at the corner. Her pupils, devoured by the thick rims of her eyelids, black as Djenne stone, were riveted on Gnagna Guisse's mouth. In her disappointment, Ngone War Thiandum's eyes flashed feverishly as she looked up, angrily, at the griot. There was no doubt. No doubt at all. Her friend, who had once been her confidant, did not understand her. The griot, by holding back, was playing a game with her. She no longer had any confidence in her. She repeated:

'You understand nothing. Nothing at all. Let me ask you, who do they accuse of being the father of the child that is to be born?'

'Who? ... There is no question at all about that. Everyone knows it is the navetanekat.'

Ngone War Thiandum buried her face in her hands and begged Yallah's pity. Choked by her suffering, she could find no words. A veil of obstinacy covered her eyes, glistening with disappointment.

'Gnagna, the truth. Only the truth. You know very well that what they say is not true. If they think it is, then they are feeding themselves on lies. The navetanekat is not the culprit. And don't say you never thought otherwise, because the navetanekat went to see your husband, Dethye Law. He came to see me, and swore he was not to blame.'

'Do you have greater faith in the words of a good-for-nothing than in those of your gueweloi-diudu?' replied Gnagna Guisse, sticking her chin out.

Together they had watched the years pass by. It was the affection that people have for friends of their own age, which is often stronger than ties of blood, that Gnagna Guisse was trying to revive, but instead she came up against the unyielding tone and look of the mother.

'I'm listening,' said Ngone War Thiandum, aggressively.
Tiny white specks gleamed in her eyes.

'I don't understand what you mean.'

'You do know, Gnagna. You do know. Before Yallah, I think
you do know.'

'I know nothing.'

'And you suspect no one? No one at all? *Oh, prudish friendship!
Bright coat on the wounded body of frankness. Oh, eyes that know, mouth
that is reluctant to hurt.*'

'No, I say.'

'It is a sin to lie. It is unfriendly to lie to me.'

Once again they faced one another. Each looked into the pool
of the other's eyes, and saw herself reflected there. In her anxiety
to hear the reply to her question, the mother's lip quivered,
almost imperceptibly. Her breath came fast, in gasps. She went
on: 'When you questioned Khar, she never said it was the navetanekat. Nor did she mention any name. Her brother Tanor beat
her black and blue, and she said nothing. The navetanekat was
driven from the village, and his field taken from him. It was a
fine field. On his own he had got rid of the thorn bushes. It had
been abandoned by everyone else because of the thorns. We
profited from his work. All the Ndiobene did. Even I blamed him.
I was glad to hear what had happened to him. And during this
time, I shared my bed with my husband, Guibril Guedj Diob.
For weeks, I saw him call Khar and speak with her. In my presence,
they shared the common dish. Oh! they only talked about things
you'd expect a father and daughter to talk about. For nine months
I was deceived. By whom? With whom? Wife and mother,
I lived with them. I did everything to find out who was the father
of her child. I begged her on my knees to tell me, I wept, and
promised her anything she wanted. In time, I would have forgotten, everyone would have forgotten. But how can anyone in
Santhiu-Niaye forget that Guibril Guedj Diob, the father of
Khar Madiagua Diob, has committed incest? He, the village
chief, the noblest descendant of the most illustrious families of
the niaye? Had he been a griot, a shoemaker, a jeweller, it would

have been understandable. Oh! forgive me, it's not you I meant. You are one of the noblest griots.'

Ngone War Thiandum stopped. The way she tried to soften and take the edge off the inflexions of her voice, the pauses between her words, all betrayed her anger.

Gnagna Guisse was quick to realize where the blame lay. She knew the pride of the Thiandum-Thiandum, their boundless pride, the absurd value they attached to their birth and which they inflicted on the whole community. Was it not one of her uncles who, after being struck in public by a toubab, by a European, had killed him and then meted out his own punishment? Their motto was: 'Rather die a thousand deaths in a thousand ways each more terrible than the other than endure an insult for a single day.' Since the most far-off times, this same clan had occupied the most coveted positions at village meetings. Gnagna Guisse herself was proud to be their genealogical griot. Guessing the fury of her guelewar's distress, she would gain her objective and get through to her with words of consolation.

Breathing heavily, Ngone War Thiandum began cursing men and life, and declared, finally, that on the judgment day she would have things to say.

'I ... .'

'You knew, didn't you?' Ngone War Thiandum tried to make her admit. She looked the griot straight in the eyes, with a hard, penetrating look, trying to read her most secret thoughts. She continued:

'You knew. How many others know? I know what is being said at the well. What shame for me and my family!'

From the other side of the bamboo partition, they could hear the voice of Guibril Guedj Diob, her husband. Ngone War Thiandum stopped talking. She lifted her head, and let her gaze wander in the distance. She was not trying to escape from her tragedy. It was now part of her, and she wanted no pity.

As they listened to Guibril Guedj Diob, they looked at one another.

'You must eat. I am going to prepare something for you.

You are my guelewar,' said Gnagna Guisse, getting up.

The mother immediately seized her wrist. 'You knew, didn't you?'

Gnagna Guisse nodded, moving away. Left alone, Ngone War Thiandum recalled all the aspects of the affair. Her growing doubts and her talks with her daughter all came back.

'Is it true that you are carrying a child?' she had asked Khar, going into her hut.

Khar Madiagua Diob had turned her eyes away. Her mother's inquisitorial look penetrated every pore of her body. She shook her head so that her mother could not see the rapid throbbing above her neck. The dark patch did not give her away.

'Tell me!'

'I am not pregnant, mother,' Khar had replied and, pretending she had some chores to do, she had fled.

Ngone War Thiandum had believed her daughter.

As the days and weeks passed, the persistent gossip about Khar had finally alarmed her. She began to spy on her daughter, watching the way she walked, the movements of her limbs, her face, her voice. In the end, she was convinced. There was no doubt! It was no use her putting on more cloths. Her hips broadened. Her belly took shape and her breasts filled out. Several times Khar Madiagua Diob had caught her mother watching her.

Then, one afternoon, as Khar Madiagua Diob was walking past, her mother suddenly put out her hand and undid the knot of the first cloth, then the second and the third, until all the cloths lay at the girl's feet. Khar Madiagua Diob had no time to pretend.

'Don't hold your belly in. If it's for my benefit, you're wasting your time. You are as full as a she-ass,' her mother had said.

Nevertheless, she went on feeling her daughter's belly with expert fingers.

'It's not possible! You don't have a husband. You really are pregnant,' she had expostulated.

Oh, maternal tenderness! Infinite goodness, how many victims have you had?

Mother and daughter looked at each other. Tears welled up

in her daughter's eyes. She fled, leaving the cloths behind.

Ngone War Thiandum had not known what to say. Her thoughts had sped confusedly in all directions. Her maternal ambition had collapsed, her dreams were destroyed, her hopes disappointed. Had she not dreamt of the day when she would lead her virgin daughter to the threshold of her husband's house? Had she not rejoiced in her anticipation of the day when she would hold up her daughter's immaculate cloth, when she would show the jewelry she had inherited from her own mother, and hand it over in public to Khar? These jewels were the pride of her lineage, the links in the chain that held it together. Had she not caressed the sweet sensation of being the mother who would endow her daughter better than any other, of celebrating a marriage that would always be remembered?

This agitated, painful monologue had taken place as the evidence of her daughter's pregnancy gained a hold on her nerves. Yet in spite of herself, Ngone War Thiandum had become reconciled to her daughter's condition. She now set about the second stage, which was to find out who was the author of this shameful deed. She had tried different approaches—concern, kindness, anger. They had only had the effect of making her failure more bitter and leaving her unhappy with her daughter's categorical refusal to say more than was displayed by the round protrusion of her belly. Worse, Khar Madiagua Diob would, at times, insolently stick out her belly.

Ngone War Thiandum unburdened herself to her husband.

'Guedj, do you know what is happening in your house?'

'I am listening.'

'Look around you.'

'For pity's sake!' Guibril Guedj Diob had implored her.

'Everyone says that your daughter, Khar Madiagua Diob, is pregnant.'

'Every week, gossip makes a girl of Santhiu-Niaye pregnant.'

Saying this, Guibril Guedj Diob had left her.

Her daughter's condition was becoming known. Suspicion fell on the navetanekat. Several times, Ngone War Thiandum went to see the young man. He always gave the same reply:

'Mother Ngone, I swear it was not me.'

'Who was it then?'

'Only Khar can say.'

Ngone War Thiandum had no alternative but to discuss it again with her husband. She did so in accordance with the accepted etiquette: she waited for complete dark, when no indiscreet ear would be lying in wait.

'You know, Guedj, that Khar is now a woman. She has been since the month of barahlu. I have asked her, but in vain. She refuses to answer.'

'If you had watched over your daughter better, nothing would have happened. She'll have her child … All right, I'll talk to her tomorrow, inchallah,' he replied, turning his back.

In the days that followed, Ngone War Thiandum found herself, as in the beginning, up against her daughter's obstinate silence. Khar Madiagua Diob's condition was food for gossip in Santhiu-Niaye. The gossip-mongers, who were always short of fodder during the navet, were delighted.

'She was seen with the navetanekat.'

'Why did she take water to him in the field?'

'Wasn't it she who washed his rags?'

'A well-born girl going with her father's servant!'

In the peinthieu, everyone discussed her case and judged it harshly.

The eldest Ndiobene, Tanor Ngone Diob, who was lucid at the time, was very angry. He discussed it with his mother.

The day's sun was growing old; the ndjiolor's rays were losing their strength. Beyond the horizon, the niaye embraced the sky. The vast expanse, with its patches of cultivated ground, seemed dull, lifeless, bleak and sad. The ash-coloured turtle-doves sang their weary notes.

Tanor Ngone Diob, in uniform—an old one bequeathed him by the kind offices of the French colonial army—took the path over the dunes, climbed them, descended them, taking care to avoid the fragile vradj bushes.

A mangy dog with long, torn ears covered in humming flies welcomed him with frightened yaps.

Atoumane, the navetanekat, warned of his presence, came to meet him.

'Peace only,' said Atoumane. (It was his day off, when he was free to work in his own field.)

'How much seed have you sown?'

The two men scanned the field, measuring with their eyes the area that had been cultivated. The navetanekat's heart beat with pride.

'Only what your father has loaned me.'

'I had something to ask you. Have you finished for today?'

Warned by his intuition, the navetanekat inwardly kept his distance. He knew that the eldest son of the ndiatigui (master) was not entirely sane.

'I was just leaving,' said the navetanekat. With a sharp whistle, Atoumane called the dog. Walking behind the ndiatigui's son, he saw him deliberately drag his boots over the groundnuts. He was tempted to say: 'Master, look where you are walking,' but he restrained himself, with a painful pull at his heart.

'Do you know why I am here?' asked Tanor Ngone Diob, a little further on.

'No, ndiatigui, no.'

'Is that true? You really don't know?'

'How can I know if you tell me nothing, ndiatigui? Perhaps there is talk in the village.'

'You take me for an idiot?' said Tanor in French.

The other looked at him open-eyed.

Tanor Ngone Diob was silent for a while. Over their heads a flock of birds flew in the direction of the sunset.

'Khar comes to see you?'

'Me? Once or twice, yes. She was going to the small field. Has something happened to her?'

'Ah!'

'Lahilah illalah!' exclaimed the navetanekat, without abandoning his reserve.

'You have slept with her?'

'Never!'

'You have made her pregnant, you bastard.'

'That's not true.'

Tanor Ngone Diob leapt at him. Atoumane jumped aside, and a chase began across the field. As he ran, Atoumane cried:

'It wasn't me! It wasn't me!'

The dog followed, barking.

Tanor Ngone Diob stopped, out of breath, shouting insults at the navetanekat. At the same time, he trampled his plants, muttering: 'It was like this in the paddy fields.' A bestial fury masked his face, and an unsatisfied gleam shone in his eyes.

Atoumane hurried off to find help to dislodge him from his field.

Accompanied by villagers, including Medoune Diob, Tanor Ngone Diob's uncle, he found Tanor had trampled most of his field.

'He's the one, the bastard. He's the one who seduced Khar,' Tanor shouted as the crowd approached.

Atoumane took to his heels once again, pursued this time by Tanor's uncle, Medoune Diob. The rest followed behind. All night they hunted him, and for several days and nights afterwards. He was never seen at Santhiu-Niaye again. All that was left of him was his mangy dog.

After this, Tanor Ngone Diob had beaten his sister Khar to make her talk. But Khar Madiagua Diob had kept silent.

'When the child is born, we'll see who it looks like,' people said, discouraged.

Others, with biting irony, retorted:

'Vah! When people live in the same place, there is a strong chance that the children will all be alike.'

Ngone War Thiandum was too obstinate to be satisfied with this. She pretended to accept it as the fruit of normal relations. With her daughter, she was cautious. In their conversation, they returned to a happy normality. Her lips said:

'Atte Yallah-la! It was the will of Yallah!"

But her instinctive desire to penetrate her daughter's secret was not far below the surface. Before, she had been afraid to go against the precepts she had been brought up to obey, so she dared not ask questions or appear suspicious. Now, with a healthy curiosity of mind, she was anxious to know and did not pay any attention to the warnings of others. Thinking was the function of the men, an iniquitous state of affairs that exasperated her. Deprived of all right to criticize or to analyse, she now revolted against an order that had been established before she was born. A sea of anger welled up and roared within her, waking and sharpening her awareness of her frustration and placing the accepted moral values in question by baring them to the light of day.

Insidiously, discreetly, she felt her way, asking indirect questions. Slowly she made progress, until, one day, without realizing it, Khar Madiagua Diob revealed the truth:

'It was my father.'

That night, and those that followed, Ngone War Thiandum did not close her eyes. She felt it was pointless to bully or beat her daughter. The responsibility for the deed had shifted and been placed on another level. 'How did it happen?' she asked herself. 'How was it that the noble blood that has flowed for centuries in the veins of Guibril Guedj Diob did not cry out? Why did his infamous deed not choke him? Had he forgotten his ancestors? How could he disgrace the honour of their names? And what will people say? It's not true! Yes, that's why, when I spoke to him about it, he jumped down my throat.' Endlessly, she returned to these thoughts. Had she not been docile, submissive? a good wife? Had she not carefully watched over her husband's conduct? These questions led to others. 'What would the champions of the moral law say now?' Had he had Khar's consent? She could neither believe nor accept that their relationship had occurred more than once. Where? Here? In the house? In the niaye? Stifled by her impotence, she blamed everyone: an attractive face, an unctuous voice, high birth, fine dress. All that had once seemed superior to her and of high moral value was merely gilt. People clad themselves in morality the better to cheat and deceive their neighbour. A man whose piety was legendary only adopted the pose so as to be better able to accomplish some unmentionable act of lust.

'Run and fetch Gnagna Guisse,' the second wife shouted, from behind the partition, to a little girl.

Ngone War Thiandum looked between the slats. The door of of the hut in which her daughter was in labour was half open.

'Go quickly.'

'Mother, here she is,' said the little girl, about to rush off.

'Khar called out. I heard her,' the second wife told Gnagna Guisse as she arrived, balancing a calebash on her head.

'I am coming,' said the griot, going towards her guelewar's hut. Ngone War Thiandum followed her.

———

THE SEASONS OF LOLI AND THORONE RELEASED THE MEN and women from their hard work in the fields. In Santhiu-Niaye, these were long, unvarying, dreary days. After the first prayer of the rising sun, some of the men would return home, others would go off into the niaye.

At yoryor, weary with inactivity and boredom, beads in hand, they returned to sit under the beintan tree, where the shoemaker-griot, Dethye Law, worked. These monotonous days of idleness encouraged conversation. The unfinished discussions of the previous navet or of earlier navets were resumed. These interminable sessions of talk enlivened the dead season. The *commandant de cercle's* visit had been announced, and was expected for the next day but one. At the entrance to the village, people were busy making a triumphal arch out of palms. This work had been left to the youngsters.

That yoryor, Baye Yamar was, as usual, the first to arrive under the tree. Dethye Law, sitting cross-legged, greeted him. They had already met at the fadyar (dawn) prayer. Baye Yamar, wearing the red chechia of a former Senegalese *tirailleur*, returned the shoemaker's greeting with two nods of the head, up and down, holding out his beads. 'I'm busy,' said his face, shaded by his thick eyebrows. Arranging his boubou, dyed a pale indigo blue, he sat on a root jutting from the ground.

The shoemaker-griot sang to himself.

The minutes passed.

'I've just been to the other side of the reed pool. I've brought back a miserable bundle of straw,' said Gornaru who, with two flips of his feet, shook off his samaras before sitting on the ground. After exchanging the morning civilities, he went on: 'I also went as far as the road, the one that is being built. The labourers told me that it is going right across the niaye.'

'Did you notice how heavy the dew was?' asked Dethye Law. His face resembled a grid, with deep incisions around his mouth opening out from his nose. The beintan tree's shadow was becoming darker.

'I even heard the call of the navet bird.'

'Me, too. I felt apprehensive when I heard it. I even asked my wife. She is usually the first to tell me about it. But everything seems topsy-turvy this year.'

'Ah, things aren't like they used to be. Yet the sun rises in the east and sets in the west. What has changed?'

Gornaru's voice was heavy. He had a bony face, with cheeks that stood out on stalks, and scaly skin, all shrivelled and rough. His eyes were red like niaye pimentos. Sitting with his legs crossed, his forearms resting on his knees, his hands hanging free, he played with the sand, sifting it from one hand to the other.

'They said the road would cross the niaye,' he repeated, as if he were telling them a secret they had not heard properly the first time. 'Keur-Malamine is going to be near the road. That's what they're saying. Perhaps that is why the toubab-commandant is coming.'

Dethye Law, his mouth full of water, spattered a piece of leather and worked it with his hands. His lower lip was still wet as he said, in his turn:

'I don't know why the toubab-commandant is coming. Apparently cars stop now at Keur-Moussa. They even have two shops where you can buy anything. Before, they were fewer than we are. Other families have come from the niaye to live with them. We should think about it. Here, there is nothing.'

'Join up with them? No one here would want that. We must go our own way,' asserted Gornaru. Then, changing the subject: 'I walked across Massar's field. It is infested with hordes of ants. I don't think anyone has cast a spell on him. Anyway, why should they?'

'What are you trying to insinuate, Gornaru?' asked Baye Yamar, who had finished his beads and was rubbing his face with them. Carefully, he replaced them in his only pocket, on his chest, and felt around the stitching with his fingers. Then he said: 'As far as I know, no one has asked for that field this year again. There has been a legal wrangle going on over the boundary for two navets. It is about time it stopped.'

'Baye Yamar, you are giving my words a meaning I did not intend.'

'I heard, Gornaru.'

'You heard wrong, if I may say so, for which I ask you to forgive me, before Yallah and before Dethye Law.'

'I beg your pardon, then.'

'So be it! May Yallah pardon us all.'

'Amine! Amine!' repeated Baye Yamar.

'I didn't see you this fadyar,' Dethye said to Gornaru, changing the subject, for he knew only too well where this effusion of good feelings would end. When a conversation began in that tone, the silence which followed was solid and long, while each chewed over his discontent. He was on the lookout for this sort of thing, and always tried to keep conversations moving. When a conversation was in full swing, he kept quiet. Dethye Law was of low caste, being a griot by birth and a shoemaker by trade. Nature, independently of our judgement and considerations, establishes its own hierarchy. Dethye Law was the bilal of the mosque, possessor of one of the finest voices for calling people to prayer. The freedom he enjoyed to speak his mind made of this tart diambur-diambur the most redoubtable of commentators. Conscious of his rank as a griot, he said what others dared not say, and everyone confided in him.

'All the same, I heard your node for the fadyar prayer. I was just leaving the village,' replied Gornaru, turning around.

On the other side of the peinthieu, someone rode by on a donkey. He wrinkled his brow and asked: 'Who's that on the donkey?'

'Have you already lost your sight? It's Amath. I know by the way he sits astride his donkey,' said Baye Yamar, with pride in his voice. 'And yet I am older than you.'

'It is true, then, that he is leaving?' asked Gornaru. He was eight years Baye Yamar's junior, in his fifties at least.

'So he says.'

'And who will look after his house, his donkeys and his fields?'

'He will do the same as all those who have left. Here's Badieye.'

Gornaru looked in the direction indicated and recognized his eternal draughts opponent. Pivoting on his buttocks, he gathered up a few sticks.

'Are you in peace, friends?' announced Badieye, with his boyish air of innocence. In his turn, he gathered up dry donkey droppings, or anything else lying around, as he talked:

'Dethye Law, have you seen Latyr go past? He is supposed to be coming back from town today.'

'I had forgotten him. It's two weeks now since he left.'

'So it is! He must be back for the toubab's visit. Unless he has found shoes for his feet in town. The old women in the town are well-preserved, they say. One of these days he will also leave never to return,' said Badieye, his hands full.

'Perhaps,' rejoined Dethye Law, sceptically.

'Eskeiye!' exclaimed Badieye, seating himself in front of Gornaru. 'So Santhiu-Niaye dies! And when is Amath leaving?'

'Who knows? Monday, they say,' replied Gornaru. 'He won't be here when the toubab-commandant arrives.'

'Next Monday? He doesn't want to pay his tax.'

'The cunning devil.'

'You wake in the morning, and there's an empty concession.

The empty sahhc collapses first, before the main hut. Then, gently, noiselessly, the roof of the main hut caves in. More silent than a grave, more open than a market place, alone and without witnesses, the main hut is consumed, night after night, in the silence of its abandonment. As if some heaven-knows-what was trying to put out the fire in some invisible hearth with equally invisible fingers. And the weeds come, growing first where feet seldom went, where only crawling babies ventured. But the part where the adults moved about keeps its marks for a long time. It is as if the grass, by refusing to grow there, hallows it. And the sand! It heaps up, no one knows how, invading the whole house. It begins its work with the hearth, once the centre and reflection of the family's security. The women and children used to glance at it furtively, silently expressing the peace in their hearts and the hope in their eyes. There, and nowhere else, is where the sand accumulates first. Then it reaches the bed, under the bed, and begins to pile up.'

Dethye Law spoke sadly, with the reserve and modesty of someone accustomed to long soliloquies and who, finding an opportunity to externalize his feelings, does so like an actor anxious for an audience. The others had listened, feeling, with each of the shoemaker-griot's words, their own anxiety at the growing number of desertions. They would have liked to speak, to express their feelings, the pain they felt in their hearts each time one of them went away, but they lacked the words. Yes! Long years of servitude break a man, deprive him of the aristocratic use of words. In other countries, the ability to embellish language is the preserve of the high-bred. But their eyes, which day after day read the disintegration of the community, were better able to speak for them. This silence, rich in unexpressed words, bound them together. They let the minutes pass, without speaking.

Gornaru broke the silence, as he drew squares in the sand for the game:

'The authorities won't do anything here, not for us. Except to suck us like tobacco. The toubab-commandant is only coming to collect the tax.'

Who said anything about the authorities?' retorted Baye
Yamar, pursing his lips. A fire that was contemptuous of the
authorities shone in his eyes, a feeling they all shared. 'My family
and I will never leave Santhiu-Niaye,' he concluded, curtly. A
look of defiance remained in his eyes.

The conversation flagged. The draughts began.

'Stick it in, up to the hilt,' cried Badieye.

'Draw it out, all covered with blood,' capped Gornaru.

'Men, I salute you,' Yaye Khuredia greeted them, relieving
herself of her basket. Her worn skin made it impossible to tell
her age. Beneath her faded cotton dress, her skin hung loose on
her bones. Every morning, under the beintan tree, she sold
different sorts of food. Fanatically superstitious, she recited
incantations to ensure a good day.

'Be careful of the centre thorn of the prickly pear, Khuredia,
it's the fruit of the devil,' Badieye teased her.

'Fruit of the devil? Perhaps. My family live on them. Yallah
has made them grow in profusion and why?'

'For the poor! Tempting the poor is satan's job.'

'Don't make me say, at my age, what I don't want to say,
Badieye, and what I never said when I was young.'

'When you were young! Ha! ha! I was already a man. Do you
remember? Well, let's forget it. Did you meet Latyr on your
way here?'

'On my way here? No. Perhaps he took another path?'

'I don't know.'

'One has to be careful of evil encounters.'

'What do you mean, Badieye? You ought to be ashamed, at
your age.'

Seated behind her display, she listened to the rude comments
of the draughts players, the yothekat. And, at each lewd remark,
she looked the other way.

'Were you the first up this morning?' Dethye asked her.

'No. I had just turned the second bend in the path of the two
palms when I saw Tanor Ngone Diob, by himself on the top of the
hill, gesticulating wildly. I saw him again just now, with palm

leaves in his hands. He was coming this way.'

'Tanor Ngone Diob! ... *Diobe duide demone tol fate fa duibame* son of Guibril Guedj Diob and Ngone War Thiandum,' intoned Badieye, going on to declaim the whole genealogy of the former combatant of Indochina and North Africa, and concluding: 'I don't know what madness drives a blind man to amuse himself by jumping from one side of a well to the other.'

'Tanor Ngone Diob is an ex-serviceman. He fought in Indochina, Morocco and Algeria. He knows how to welcome the toubab-commandant. Tell, what is the fruit that never falls and is never ripe?'

The two yothe players burst out laughing.

'Astafourlah!' cried Yaye Khuredia.

The sun filled the square. The white sand was dazzling. They closed their eyes as little as possible in order to penetrate the haze rising from the ground.

> *O! près de ma b'onde qu'i' fait bon*
> *Bo' bo' bo' bo' dormir.*

With this refrain, Tanor Ngone Diob appeared at the other end of the square. Singing at the top of his voice, he came from where the toubab-commandant's triumphal arch was being erected. A crowd of children trotted in his wake. He wore the camouflage uniform of a parachutist, and on his dirty, frizzy hair sat the cap of a soldier of the French Expeditionary Corps. His boots were without laces, there were no socks on his feet. From his belt hung a parachutist's knife.

When he reached the elders, he clicked his heels together and gave a military salute.

'At ease, adjutant,' ordered Dethye.

Tanor Ngone Diob made an about-turn and addressed the invisible soldiers:

'Slo ... pe ar ... ms! Dis ...miss!'

He walked playfully up to the shoemaker.

'Have you slept well?'

'I was on guard duty. There were Vietcong everywhere,' replied the ex-soldier, gripping the handle of his knife. His eyes rolled from left to right, then he stopped his mimicry and looked at the trader:

'I've seen you twice this morning. You're following me about.'

Trembling, she drew in her neck and tried to make herself small. A shiver of fear ran down her spine. Dethye Law looked at her, as if to say:

'He won't hurt you. Don't answer him.'

'Old cow! Dried up piece of fish! Rusty bit of iron! Empty well! She-devil! I see you! Ya! ya! ah! ah! ah!' he bellowed, baring his teeth menacingly.

Cowed, Yaye Khuredia got up to go. Tanor Ngone Diob, armed with a fistful of sand, ordered:

'Battery! Fire!'

His mad laughter stopped all talk. A crowd gathered at a distance, laughing.

'Go home,' Dethye called to them, trying to make them go away. 'Calm yourself, Tanor! It is hot.'

'Dul! Go to hell! Bite your rotten skin! Arse-skin! Donkey's arse! The donkey's dead! Dead! It'll fart no more!'

Laughter broke out on all sides.

Tanor Ngone Diob, happy to be the centre of attention, executed the steps of a tango, singing to himself:

Li plus b'o de touss lis tango que z'ai dansé·
C'é a lui que z'ai dansé dans ton bras.

He re-arranged his uniform, stretched his neck and bowed to an imaginary partner. He stood aside to let her pass, extending his right arm, bent at the elbow. He took his imaginary partner in his arms and turned, turned, accompanying himself with his song.

Then his mood changed. He stopped short, yelling:

'*Comados! Z'armes!*'

He stood six or seven kids in a line.

'For ... ward ... mar ... ch! Lef' right, lef' right.'

He followed behind. Further on, he took up his refrain, making the children repeat it after him:

O! prés de ma b'onde qu'i fait bo.

'Eskeiye Yallah! It's the day of the ravanes, the titular genies,' said Yaye Khuredia, returning to her place. 'Such good stock! Eskeıye Yallah! Who could have foreseen this when he left for his military service? Life is nothing!'

'Life is nothing? Life is everything,' said Palla, approaching the yothekat. 'Say to a true believer: "I hope you will see paradise." Straight away, he will answer: "Amine!" Hope that he will die, and straight away he will run from you as he runs from death. Yet, no one will enter paradise alive.' He added: 'Tanor is preparing to welcome the commandant. To think he has such good blood in his veins! And now ...'

'And now?' Dethye queried.

Yaye Khuredia took up the cudgel:

'Why do you defend that family, Dethye Law? Do you think, griot as you are, that your son will marry one of their daughters?'

'And do you think I would give my son my consent if he expressed the desire to do so?'

'Why, then ...?'

'Woman, your age has taught you nothing.'

'It beats me,' said Palla, crouching with his head between his hands. 'I never understood, anyway. I don't dare believe what people are saying.'

'Eh, Palla, go somewhere else. Don't sit here shouting in our ears,' Badieye said to him, scratching his calves. His nails left whitish lines on his skin where he had scratched it.

'You two always have something to shout about,' retorted Palla.

'We shout, but it is only between ourselves.'

'What are people saying?' asked Baye Yamar. 'What are people saying, Palla?'

'I don't know,' Palla replied.

'Why bother trying to show the sun to him who refuses to see it at midday?' added Yaye Khuredia, chasing the flies that were settling on her wares.

'If you have to see in order to believe,' rapped out Dethye Law.

'I can't understand, Dethye, why you take sides with the Ndiobene,' said Palla, leaving the yothekat. 'As soon as they are mentioned, you are like pimento.' When he was at a safe distance, he turned his gravelly face towards Dethye:

'It's your stupidity, all of you, that compels me to answer you. Every one of you knows what is going on. But you are only satisfied when, like birds of prey, your beaks are rummaging in someone else's guts.'

'Everything that is possible is matter for commentary.'

'Except, Palla, when ...'

'Dethye Law, spare me your vulgarities,' interrupted Palla. He took out an old clay pipe and filled it. He had flat feet, his toes were all split by jiggers.

'Or what you don't want to hear.'

There was a pause.

The sun poured out its flow of mercury.

The 'lef' right, lef' right' approached.

'Section, halt,' ordered Tanor Ngone Diob. The children stopped. Tanor Ngone Diob fished some sweets from his pocket and distributed them among the scrambling children. His face covered in perspiration, the ex-soldier lay down on the ground, facing the shoemaker.

'You're sweating,' said Dethye Law

'It's all for the commandant! Soldiers must sing on inspection day.'

The young man smiled, but Dethye Law's face remained stern.

'I want a gree-gree,' said Tanor Ngone Diob, breaking the silence.

'A gree-gree? What for?'

Tanor Ngone Diob elbowed himself nearer. His fingers touched one of the pots standing in front of the craftsman. A silent smile spread to the corners of his eyes.

Dethye Law repeated his question.

Curious, old Yaye Khuredia came nearer. She jumped. Tanor Ngone Diob had her by the ankle, and she fell full length onto the ground. She screamed. Before the men could come to her aid, the ex-soldier was covering her with sand, insulting her all the while. A fiendish laugh came into his eyes. Covered in sand, Yaye Khuredia had lost her head-scarf. She shouted insults at him.

'How low you have fallen,' she screamed.

'Macou! Silence!' yelled Tanor Ngone Diob, his knife unsheathed and held in combat position.

'Sit up! You know he is harmless.'

'He, harmless? Don't exaggerate, Dethye Law. You are waiting for him to hurt someone before you will agree like everybody else that he is ...'

'Palla, I did not say he was not mad. I said he was harmless.'

'What about the time when he attacked the imam?'

'The imam? That's another story.'

'Story for story, he is mad. I say so again. And I swear before Yallah that the day he touches any of my family will be a day to be seen.'

'That day, you will know! Have you seen a clod of earth strike a stone?'

'Is that what you think? It's true, your wife is their griot. They are all depraved. A father who ...'

'That's enough,' intervened Baye Yamar firmly. He had stood up to give himself more authority. His chechia made him seem taller than he was. 'You would think none of you were fathers of families. These days, it seems we can't discuss things like friends. Some subjects one is wise not to mention, even in anger.'

'The whole of Santhiu-Niaye, and even people outside, know that Khar Madiagua Diob is pregnant by ...'

'Enough!'

'They call themselves guelewars!' muttered Palla, sitting down again.

Tanor Ngone Diob re-sheathed his knife.

O! près de ma b'onde qu'i fait bo.

Singing his refrain, he took himself off.

They were, in fact, good men, who got on together without standing on ceremony. Mostly they controlled their irritation and caste prejudices, but sometimes they came to the surface and overflowed.

In silence, they watched Tanor Ngone Diob disappear with his song.

Carrying his dove-coloured shot silk sunshade, Guibril Guedj Diob appeared, accompanied by his younger brother, Medoune Diob. Tanor Ngone Diob's bestial cry could be heard in the distance.

'Eskeiye Yallah! Poor people.'

'Which people?' asked Gornaru.

'All the Ndiobene,' said Palla.

'I greet you all,' said Medoune Diob, sitting down next to Baye Yamar. 'Has the imam passed by?'

'I haven't seen him yet.'

'I think I saw him at the entrance to the village.'

'Thank you,' he replied, getting up. He was sure they had just been discussing the Ndiobene. He moved off in the direction of the entrance to the village.

The sun rose higher. Its hind-quarters low, its ears drooping, the dog came and lay down next to the trader, resting its jaws on the ground. A swarm of flies collected on its head.

Only the comments of the yothe players under the beintan tree continued to fly.

――――――――――

FOR AS LONG AS SANTHIU-NIAYE CONTINUES TO RISE FROM the nights of time, its name will be associated with the Ndiobene. Like his fellow villagers, the head of the Ndiobene, Guibril Guedj Diob, went regularly to the mosque, the small enclosure in the middle of the peinthieu. When the pregnancy of his daughter, Khar Madiagua Diob, became common knowledge, a discussion was initiated by his younger brother, Medoune Diob. In all the annals of the elders' experience, such a delicate situation had never haunted people's minds more. Having completed the formulas of politeness, Medoune Diob repeated:

'My brother is responsible for his daughter's condition.'

'Ought he to die? Or should he be expelled from our village?'

asked Massar. His head was flat on top, elongated behind, and his eyes were running with pus: everything about him demonstrated the effects of too much intermarriage. Without waiting for a reply, he went on:

'According to Koranic law, Guibril Guedj Diob deserves to die. This is what the scriptures say. But have the penalties demanded by the scriptures for infringement of the law ever been applied here?'

'Massar, speak for yourself,' retorted Medoune Diob.

'I am asking the imam,' said Massar, turning towards him.

The imam, with the stern face of the mystic, was saying his beads. Assembled there were the most enlightened minds of Santhiu-Niaye: five men.

'And what does our adda say?'

Baye Yamar looked at each of them in turn, and went on:

'The adda has always been the first rule in the lives of our fathers. If that rule is broken, it deserves either death or expulsion from the community.'

'If we are to preserve the adda and give the example,' said Medoune Diob, 'if we are to vindicate the honour of our community, the couple ought to be punished. The Koran is clear about that. And we are all Muslims here. The punishment must be carried out in public, in front of everyone, or the guilty party must be thrown into a well and the opening blocked with stones.'

'Every crime must have its penalty. That is quite true. Have we ever punished or expelled anyone for infringing the adda, or for failing to respect someone else's property?'

Medoune Diob felt a gnawing at his heart as he listened to Dethye Law. For months they had been clashing with one another. Now, he controlled an impulse to hurl in his face: 'There is no one of your nawle, of your social rank here.' When it had been discussed who should attend the meeting, he had been opposed to Dethye Law's presence.

'The case is clear. Yallah knows I love my brother. Not only because he is my brother, and like everyone else, a believer, but our inescapable duty to consider the honour of the community guides me, and ought to guide you as well. Guibril Guedj Diob's infamous behaviour brings shame on the whole of Santhiu-Niaye. Wherever we go, even our children, we will be pointed at. Even those who are not of our nawle will despise us.'

'That is true,' capped Amath.

'May I leave?' asked Dethye Law, placing his ancient fez on his head.

'Why?'

'Because, Baye Yamar, I have not come here to be insulted.'

'Who has said anything to insult you?'

'I know the meanings of words. I know I was born a griot, but I'll never be an accomplice, not even morally.'

'Dethye Law, don't leave with your heart on fire. A discussion has never been held without you. You are our griot, after all.'

'I ask the assembly's pardon. I know my place in our community. However, one thing is certain. When it is a question of speaking the truth, or of seeking it, there is no nawle. It is a known fact that many of my caste have been murdered in the cause of truth. It is true that Guibril Guedj Diob deserves to die. It was the rule of our fathers and of our grandfathers, in the days when the essence of nobility depended on the way one lived, not on self-display. We can call to mind the names of many who put an end to their lives for acts less than the one we are discussing today. They were guelewar, men whose praises were sung by my father and his father, not to give pleasure, but to impress on their hearers the meaning of duty and dignity. Nowadays, people do not conduct themselves in this way. But truth belongs to all times, and will do so even after we are dead.'

Dethye Law paused. He lowered his face, and his body swayed gently. Then he went on, in an even voice:

'I wonder,' said Kotje-Barma at a similar meeting, 'what one ought to think of old men who marry girls the same age as their daughters?'

There was a heavy silence for some seconds. Only the regular clicking of the imam's beads could be heard. He uncrossed his legs, and began in the Arabic tone of voice he affected:

'I do not share Kotje-Barma's reservations. Are we to believe that an old man who marries a girl the same age as his daughter is committing incest?'

'A girl the same age as your daughter, a girl who has played in your home with your daughter and whom, yesterday, you called "my child," a girl whose parents said to her: "Go and tell your father such and such", a girl you baptized, in marrying that girl you are marrying your daughter.' Dethye Law looked defiantly at the imam, furrowing the coal-black skin of his brow.

The imam held the centre bead of his rosary between two fingers and lowered his eyelids, his lips moving imperceptibly. Then, opening his eyes, he said:

'To all appearances, and looked at from a distance in this way, such behaviour is morally abnormal. But I hasten to add that no sariya or rysala supports this. There have been plenty of holy men who have had wives the same age as their daughters.'

His eyes lit up with the satisfaction that sometimes comes to dull minds reduced too long to a state of inferiority. With a studied, trenchant calm, the imam returned to his beads.

'That is true. More than a few great men have had as second, third, or fourth wife the daughter of one of their disciples. This was agreed from the outset between the two men, between the father of the girl and the future son-in-law. And the daughter, being submissive, obeyed. The conduct of a holy man is not open to discussion. Between the absolution of a marriage and sin of the flesh, there is the whole niaye. I said just now—no, I asked, whether Guibril Guedj Diob ought to die or be banished from our community. What is it we want to preserve? The purity of our body's blood? The purity of our moral blood? And, placing myself—Yallah is my witness—on the strict level of the teaching of the sariya, I ask you this: Have we at any time punished anyone, man or woman, because he has violated the holy scriptures here, among us?'

Massar waited for someone to reply.

The rivalry evident in the learning of Massar and the imam went back three years. On the death of the previous imam, the two men, in an intense, silent struggle, had each claimed the honour. They would receive no material benefit from it, but both knew that whoever held the office would have considerable influence in the community.

'Among us, then,' Massar went on, wiping the pus from his eyes, 'the scriptures are a dead letter. For, never in this village, nor in the whole of Senegal, where mosques nevertheless proliferate, not once have the penalties laid down by the holy scriptures been carried out. Go and see the authorities! We respect them and we cherish them; that seems to be all. That leaves us with the adda, the heritage of our fathers.'

'So we leave Guibril Guedj Diob alone, then?' demanded Medoune Diob. 'Our children will never to able to look one another in the eyes again.'

'Yallah has given me a voice to call his faithful. I thank him! Alhamdoulillah! I admit here and now that my knowledge of Arab literature is very limited. I shed tears every night because of it. On the other hand, I console myself—far be from me the sin of pride—saying: 'Yallah sees into our hearts and understands all the languages of the spirit.' I speak therefore for the adda, since I am the only griot here. You remember the tale of our childhood. Like Inekeïv, I cannot read. I do not know who we fear the most. Men? Yallah? A few months ago, several of us believed that the navetanekat, Atoumane, had committed the crime. Convinced by Medoune Diob and Guibril Guedj Diob, you wanted to wipe away the affront with blood, driving the navetanekat from the village. The Ndiobene had all profited from his labour and sweat. Did they call us together, as we are today, to ask us our advice? Yet the navetanekat swore he wasn't to blame. It made no difference. He even sought the intervention of the imam who is here now. What did he advise him to do?'

Dethye Law paused to draw breath. His gaze met the imam's. They looked at each other for a while. Dethye Law went on:

'What did the imam say to the navetanekat when he placed his confidence in him as spiritual leader, as Yallah's representative and the representative of us all? Nothing ... Yes, he said to him:

'My son, have faith in Yallah.' The navetanekat's hope turned to bitter disappointment. We know how he struggled in that field we had abandoned because of the thorn bushes. Enough said about that … Taking care not to be seen, he came to me. I kept him in my house for two days. I went to see Medoune Diob myself. But he was more unyielding than his elder brother Guibril Guedj Diob. Their son, Tanor Ngone Diob, in his moments of lucidity, went off to trample the field. Only Khar Madiagua Diob refused to accuse the navetanekat. Nobody wanted to believe her either. Now we can understand her. Can a daughter declare publicly: "The child I am carrying is my father's"? And you remember the night the village hunted the man? If I refuse to agree to punish Guibril Guedj Diob, it is not because I approve of incest, here or anywhere else; there is another reason. Our inability to recognize the truth does not come from our minds, but rather from the fact that we accord too much consideration to birth and wealth and also, sometimes, because we lack the courage to speak out. Between man and Yallah, I choose Yallah. Between Yallah and the Truth, I am for the Truth. Medoune Diob has something else at the back of his mind.'

'That is not true,' interrupted Medoune, vehemently.

Everyone began talking at once.

'Shout, and the truth hides itself. Remain silent, and the truth becomes hard and turns to stone,' Massar pronounced, sententiously.

'Let him finish! We have the time. If it isn't during this loli, it will be during the next,' said Baye Yamar, restoring order.

'I repeat, Medoune Diob is more concerned about the succession of the Ndiobene than about punishment. The fact that a person is of low caste has never been a hindrance to speaking the truth,' Dethye Law concluded.

'I leave you, Dethye Law. Yallah will judge us. I see this affair has been brought down to the level of the Ndiobene. I ask you to forgive me, as Yallah forgives those who offend him.'

With these words, Medoune Diob rose and left.

'I had not thought of all that,' added Baye Yamar, also leaving, accompanied by the imam.

The others, too, left.

And, for some weeks, without conniving together, all those who frequented the mosque tacitly agreed to exclude Guibril Guedj Diob. During the prayer, no one would sit next to him. When Guibril Guedj Diob placed his slippers at the entrance, the others would remove theirs. One day, at the tacousan prayer, they all walked out of the mosque, leaving him alone.

He was no longer invited to the discussions.

Of his own accord, he stopped coming to prayers, or to sit under the beintan tree. Carrying his sunshade, he went off on his own.

The niaye was white hot, empty. The sand shimmered on the dunes. On the horizon, a cloud of moving waves.

In the village, everyone was resting, overcome by the intense, torrid midday heat. The fowls stood on one leg up against the palisades, their beaks open.

Only Dethye Law was working. He was watching for the sun to begin declining, to sing the node for the tisbar prayer. Everything was like on a postcard, still and lifeless.

The dog shook its head lazily. The swarm of flies rose up, then returned to rest on its torn ears. Sleepily, it closed its eyes, indifferent to the flies. A couple of donkeys, their front legs tied together, hobbled to the shade.

Dethye Law stood up and walked out of the strip of shade. He inspected the edge of the shade with a dubious air, screwing his eyes to measure the curve of the sun. Then, placing the fingers of his right hand together, he bent them in half. They projected their shadow onto his palm: it was time for the node, the call to prayer.

———

AT THE CALL TO PRAYER, NGONE WAR THIANDUM HAD gone into the niaye. She had returned unseen. Back in the Ndiobene

concession, she sat down under the nebedaye, on the look-out for
Gnagna Guisse's arrival, while she listened for sounds from Khar
Madiagua's hut. She had mastered her anger. The child would
be born that evening, Gnagna Guisse had said. Mentally, she
counted the months: bara-helu, kor, korite, digui-tabaski, tabaski,
tam-haret, digui-gamu, gamu, raki-gamu—nine months. A feeling
of satisfaction, subtle as the scent of Segwen incense, came over her.
No woman on her mother's side had ever had an abnormal consti-
tution. She wondered what her husband's reaction would be.
Would he be able to live with his child? In the same house as the
daughter—mother of his child? In the same village? In the same
country? Live with them? With his other wives? And herself,
mother and grandmother, how would she carry out her conjugal
duties? There were no answers to any of these questions. Even
when she was dead, she thought to herself, she would not enjoy the
peace of death; she would keep rising from her grave. Would not
people say as her daughter went by:

'That's Khar Madiagua Diob, Ngone War Thiandum's
daughter. She had her first child by her father.'

Like termites eating away the inside of wood, a similar devasta-
tion had taken place in her. Ngone War Thiandum did not see
the chicken scratching and pecking as it came nearer her foot.
She gave a wild, fierce cry, raising her hand to her face in fear,
her mouth open. The terrified chicken ran off, flapping its wings.

She suddenly shut her mouth; a fly had almost flown into it.
Calm again, she heard Guibril Guedj Diob's voice. He was
scolding a little boy. Unable to resist, she looked between the slats
of the bamboo palisade. Guibril Guedj Diob's shadow fell dark at
her feet. She could only see part of him. A voice she knew, whose
every nuance she could interpret, its joys, its sorrows, its near
successes, its complete failures, its sincere communion, the acts
of piety hurriedly performed ...

Gnagna Guisse caught her unawares. She started, turning away
from the screen. She looked into the griot's eyes. A hostile silence
lay between them.

'I am the victim, you are the outsider,' said the look in the mother's eyes.

Hurt as she was by this unspoken reproof, Gnagna Guisse suppressed her thoughts. As she had done earlier that morning, she gave way. Immediately, they fell into lively conversation, in order to avoid the real subject. They recalled happily the family cycles of the past, of their youth. They had been privileged, their's had been an enviable time. In those days, the people of Santhiu-Niaye had been gay. There was a tinge of nostalgia in both their voices. Although of different rank, they were two women from the same world. They carefully avoided mentioning its defects and vices. Deliberately steering clear of them, they extolled its virtues. But even so, the urge to embellish by exaggeration could not exclude from their minds the violence that had been done to the moral law.

Talking about the season that was finishing and the season that was approaching, Gnagna Guisse explored the lie of the land again. Ngone War Thiandum spoke with her lips only. Her inner aridity had transformed her gestures into those of a statue. Her fingers kept time with her words, as she tapped the beads of her rosary, which she had wound round her wrist. The griot was wondering, too, whether she had done right. The words of the sage ran through her mind: 'Any truth that divides and brings discord among the members of the same family is false. The falsehood that weaves, unites and cements people together is truth.' Gnagna Guisse contented herself with this justification of her silence. She was relieved to see that, in spite of the incest and the effects of her sleepless nights, the mother's heart was emptying itself of its gall. But the pride of the Thiandum-Thiandum and its passive violence were still gathered at the corners of her mouth.

'Tonight, inchallah, a stranger will be in our midst,' said Gnagna Guisse, watching for the effect of her words.

'She has said nothing?'

'Nothing.'

'I want you to give her my jewelry. I inherited it from my mother, and she from her mother. I want the jewelry to be for the child, to make him a man. I want it to be a boy.'

She paused and, in her imagination, she saw the boy grown to manhood, clad in the dignity of a man. With him would begin another life, onto which would be grafted the unhappy lot of all men, renewing and fulfilling it.

'This jewelry is for the child, to help him become a man,' said Ngone War Thiandum. 'I want it to be a boy,' she repeated to herself. 'Perhaps—it's certain (after a moment's reflection)—the child won't have a family name. Let her call him Vehi-Ciosane Ngone Thiandum. I am the sole bearer of the name Thiandum. I bequeath it to him.'

Gnagna Guisse listened, but voiced no opinion … The jewelry was usually displayed on a girl's wedding day; it was also the stamp of a well-off guelewar family. It was then worn by the daughter at important ceremonies. She in turn handed it down to her descendants. Ngone War Thiandum's gesture was a departure from custom: the jewelry was passing into different hands and acquiring a new function. It was an unselfish gesture that recalled the glorious past of the Thiandum-Thiandum whose gueweloi-diudu Gnagna Guisse was. She was tempted to sing out her praises, but restrained herself from an untimely display.

The muezzin, Dethye Law, called the third node of the day: the tacousan prayer.

They rose together and entered Ngone War Thiandum's hut.

━━━━━━

AFTER THE TACOUSAN PRAYER, BADIEYE AND GORNARU had hurried back to their game of yothe. There were several onlookers, and the game was a close one.

'In you go!' grunted Gornaru, as he placed a 'nail', commenting: 'It is like when you have a boil on your backside, sitting is uncomfortable, whether you bend over or lodge it in a hollow before you sit down'.

'An unsuitable position for a suitor visiting his future in-laws,' capped Semu, taking his place.

Palla and Massar arrived from the mosque. Massar's hair was wet. Then came the others, in a group with the imam.

Between tacousan and timis, the cordiality and friendliness of the talk was mingled with personal and family tensions. The discussion would follow a line, broken from time to time by long silences; then it would start up again, often getting hopelessly involved.

'What do you say?'

'I say that yothe is a game of satan,' said the imam, turning to face Baye Yamar. He was resting on his elbows and watching the children in the distance as they dragged a recalcitrant donkey. 'You have barely finished saying your beads and you are back at your game.'

'It passes the time.'

'That's exactly what the trouble is! That time should be dedicated to Yallah. Moreover, your language is coarse.'

'That is only for the malaika. For those who have no desires, no family, no sex. I need no protector to stand between Yallah and us—myself, I mean. What I do, I do openly.'

'What others do in secret, Yallah will judge.'

'Leave him to judge me then.'

Saying this, Badieye stretched his neck, concentrated for a moment, and then, aloud:

'When you make love to a woman, either she loves you or is calculating the value of your harvest.'

Amath, who was one of his supporters, seized Badieye's wrist and added:

'True! When you have an old woman in cold weather, you warm her with your body or with firewood.'

'Those two activities are not everlasting occupations. In both of them, you lose your skin,' capped Badieye, digging his stick sharply into the ground.

There was a noisy outcry.

'You will never dare return to that hut,' said Gornaru, and, in his turn, he commented: 'Eating flesh, mounting flesh, and putting flesh inside flesh.'

And, with a sudden move, he whipped out two sticks and placed his donkey dropping.

'Astafourlah! Astafourlah!' repeated Massar, seizing Palla's forearm. Palla straightened himself, stretching his back. Massar declaimed the law in Arabic and Wolof: 'Holy Writ alone contains the truth.'

The yothekat turned to face the attack of the preachers, the imam and Massar.

'Each of us, like everyone else, will be alone in his grave. There he will answer only for his acts and his words,' declared Gornaru and, pulling Badieye, he said: 'Don't listen to them.'

Badieye, voluble, returned blow for blow.

'And Amath's departure?'

'Inchallah, I shall leave,' began Amath, not very pleased to see his departure raised again. 'I don't want to be here when the toubab-commandant arrives. I am leaving with my family. My children are grown up and ready to marry. It is Yallah's will that I only have daughters. I can't keep paying their tax.'

'If I understand you, no one here is worthy of your daughters, no one is worthy to marry them?' queried Baye Yamar.

'Me?' shouted Amath, nettled, his hand on his chest. 'Me? Who said so? If either of my daughters wants to marry one of you, we'll celebrate the union tonight. That's not why I am leaving. I am leaving because of the tax. I haven't paid it for nearly two years now.'

'Choose one of us. That's how it was done before. Since when is the initiative left to one's daughters?'

'I have always said that my daughters would decide for themselves, Baye Yamar.'

'So, then, it's your daughters who don't want us?'

'I know nothing about that. It is something I have never discussed with them.'

'Perhaps your daughters think we are too old?'

Amath preferred to keep quiet on this subject.

'Where are you going?'

Palla had finished. Massar's bald, bumpy, chocolate-coloured head stood out further than ever on his neck.

'I have relatives at Thiès. We think we'll eventually go to Ndakaru (Dakar), where I'll find work, inchallah.'

'Ndakaru! There is nothing at Ndakaru except too many people and beggars from all over.'

'You'll be an outsider there. The people in the towns have neither faith nor honour. It's as it is among the animals of the niaye. The strongest eats the weakest. There, the enterprising live off the careless. No one has time to concern himself seriously with Yallah. Old men like us are no longer the leaders. They only mark time.'

The imam spoke with authority.

'I have heard worse than that,' added Palla. 'It's not like it is here.'

'True, it is not like it is here. We have been waiting two weeks for Latyr. Some people need candles, some need soap, some need sugar, and a hundred and one other things. He ...'

'Dethye Law, do you think that in the towns these things are free for the taking?'

'No, Baye Yamar, I don't. Seeing them helps one to hope, it feeds and strengthens the will. For it is our hope in paradise that sustains us.'

'You'd do better to chew your skins,' interrupted the imam, who had been waiting a long time for the opportunity to humiliate the shoemaker.

'Diam! Peace! There is nothing, no more peace, then. Am I condemned never to open my mouth again?'

'We know what you are driving at with your sarcastic innuendos, Dethye Law.'

'Alhamdoulillah! ... Such wit!'

'Dethye Law, you have work to do. Get on with it. We were talking to Amath.'

'Palla, you know I have to leave Santhiu-Niaye. I don't want to seem to be running away, or to leave behind me the impression I am running away. Because of the tax, yes.'

'You are abandoning your family graves, that is what you are doing. Have any of those who have left ever been back, just once? No. You were born here. The niaye is peopled with the bones of your family. You are going into exile because you have allowed your children to gain an ascendancy over you. As for the tax; we will all give what we have.'

As he spoke, Palla squatted down, sharpening his knife on the heel of his samara. He spoke with a strong throaty accent.

'Your daughters are right. I agree with them. On a vast, bare stretch of land planted only with stumps, one doesn't wait for the middle of the day. One needs shade to shelter when the road is long,' was Dethye Law's opinion.

'Amath, don't listen to Dethye Law. If our village is like it is, it is the will of Yallah. All else is pride,' rejoined the imam.

'Let us leave Yallah where he is. We'll talk about him when it is his time.'

'Astafourlah! You blaspheme, Dethye Law,' said Baye Yamar, who had come to succeed Massar. His hair was wet, too. Seated at Palla's feet, he went on: 'All this is the result of spiritual sloth. It is idleness that leads to words like these.'

'I think the opposite myself. Yallah doesn't like narrow minds. They're like water that doesn't flow. Everyone knows that if water doesn't flow, it becomes stagnant. It becomes poisonous. In spite of its apparent cleanness, it eats away the earth that holds it. Hence the sterility of the earth and of the human spirit.'

The descendant of old aristocratic stock, with a sound religious upbringing, Baye Yamar had nothing of the shoemaker's critical spirit. The contempt with which this man of inferior caste filled him during the discussion sessions confirmed him in his fear that the adda was dying. Contemptuously, he said: 'Truly, your language is worthy only of your griot's rank.'

'The refusal to see or hear the truth when one is not able to grasp it for oneself or to make it one's own is a sign that one is less than a griot,' Dethye Law objected strongly, with no trace of mildness in his words.

Palla, the hairdresser, let go of Baye Yamar's head in his annoyance.

'Dethye Law, can't you take your shoemaker's language elsewhere? Leave Baye Yamar alone.'

'The inferiority of his reflections attaches me to him.'

Someone gave a hungry man's laugh, like the bursting of a calebash at midday. It was Biram, displaying his rotten teeth. Looking up, his attention was caught by Amath's elbow: it resembled a hunk of bread. For a moment, he gazed at it.

The noise from the yothe players drowned all conversation. Badieye leant to one side, unstuck his left buttock and gently broke wind. Then, glancing sheepishly, discreetly at each in turn, he finally said:

'Alhamdoulillah!'

'A bone in the house, who's it for?' inquired Gornaru.

'For the head of the concession,' someone replied.

'No, for the youngest wife,' said someone else.

The conversation split into groups. Amath had gone to sit in front of the shoemaker, and asked him for some thongs.

'Take some, but don't lose my awl. I would have to go all the way to Thiès for another.'

'What do you take me for?'

'For someone who is leaving.'

'That's true.'

Amath got up and went over to join the imam's group. Massar was talking:

'Dethye Law can tell us. His wife is there. But he won't.'

'I won't be here for the baptism,' said Amath.

'Decidedly, you push your cruelty so far as to tickle a corpse,' said the imam.

'It will have to have a name, all the same,' said Massar.

'If it's a boy, will you be its godfather?' asked the imam.

'I think children of that kind generally have a dead godfather.'

'A discreet way of getting out of it.'

'Would you accept, if it is a boy?'

Loud cries came from the yothekat. Gornaru had just won. Badieye was saying:

'I must go and wash.'

The sun, in the last stages of its decline, had embraced the whole niaye, bathing the horizon in a saffron-coloured water. The shady areas were spreading.

Dethye Law rose to his feet, stretched with a feeling of sensual pleasure, then went off in the direction of the mosque. He looked towards the setting sun, half-closed his hand again, then, facing east, he cupped his hands on each side of his mouth and in a rising voice sang out the call to prayer.

Immediately, all was quiet. The cry spiralled upwards.

———

AFTER SUNRISE, GNAGNA GUISSE HURRIED FROM CONCES-
sion to concession, the bearer of a message. In each, the formal greetings were pronounced as if in secret. In a voice of consterna-tion, she whispered with the master of the house; their faces, the colour of wrinkled, crumpled tobacco leaves, were aghast. And, when she left, people commented:

'Well, she has found peace of mind. This world was not a place for her.'

With these two sentences, unanimity was restored.

People set off along the paths leading to the Ndiobene con-cession. The old women, wearing their ceremonial head-cloths, walked in procession between the palisades, whispering together.

'With such a weight on her heart, her blood turned sour. Thank Yallah for calling her to him,' said one of them piously.

'Khar Madiagua Diob was delivered like an animal last night,' revealed another, with an air of assurance, proud to be the first to tell the news.

'What did you say?' asked a woman, leaving the person she was talking to.

'As the sun hangs over us, I tell you.'

'It is the night giving birth to the sun.'

'What did she have?'

'No one knows. She is at Dethye Law's house. People are saying it is a monster.'

'She could only have a monster. Yallah has lost patience with our times. And now she has killed her mother. She would have done better to have died in labour.'

'Rather, Guibril Guedj Diob should have died.'

'I can't imagine how a man like him could have acted the way he did.'

'His ancestors must want to leave their graves.'

'Where is our world going?'

The old women stood in a line on one side of the Ndiobene concession, gossiping.

'And Khar?'

'She is at Dethye Law's house. No one will go and look for her there. As you know, when you cross the threshold of that house, no one has any right over you,' said Yaye Khuredia, who was suitably dressed for the occasion.

'And Guibril Guedj Diob?'

'He has gone to the cemetery.'

'That's the least he could do! In his place, I wouldn't have gone. Or else I wouldn't come back from the cemetery. When you are a guelewar, you don't outlive such an act,' said the third woman, facing the entrance of the hut.

'What dishonour! I am sure Ngone War Thiandum took her own life.'

'Rather die a thousand deaths in a thousand ways each more terrible than the other than endure an insult for a single day. That is their motto, the motto of the Thiandum-Thiandum. She has not failed the tradition.'

'That is what everyone is saying. She could not overcome her shame. She was a real Thiandum. The last of her line. Her blood has spoken,' said Yaye Khuredia, speaking again. 'Guibril Guedj Diob's crime will never be forgotten. A shame!'

'A shame? ... a depraved act, yes.'

'It's moral murder. Khar Madiagua Diob has killed her mother. No one here will marry her. Even if there were only old men left. Can you see my daughter as her co-wife? Never!'

'It's Guibril Guedj Diob's fault. Khar Madiagua Diob has

done nothing.'

'How do you mean, she has done nothing?' asked Yaye Khuredia, straightening her flat chest as she turned towards the woman who had spoken. 'How do you mean, she has done nothing? How often did she sleep with her father? It was in the niaye that they performed their shameless acts, under the eyes of Yallah and his malaika.'

'May Yallah forgive us such behaviour,' objected a woman. 'Perhaps her father forced her?'

'Forced her? Rubbish! How can you force a young girl? She could have shouted. I maintain she consented. Like a satan, she tempted her father.'

'She must not live here any longer. We must make life impossible for her.'

An old woman of Yaye Khuredia's generation made her entry. She excused herself profusely for being late. Yaye Khuredia invited her to join them. Quickly she put her in the picture, and continued:

'If Khar Madiagua Diob stays, she could be a bad example for our daughters. All the young men are in the village. And the fathers risk being tempted away from Yallah's path.'

'When I was very young, I heard of a case of incest. The man was buried alive. I heard of it from my mother. But I never thought I'd live to see it myself. Indeed, to whom must I extend my condolences?' concluded the latest arrival, wedged between Yaye Khuredia and the other woman.

'To whom? Guibril Guedj Diob? Khar Madiagua Diob? Perhaps to the second veudieu? I can see her over there, with her affected air. She must be rejoicing now.'

'And Tanor Ngone Diob?'

'The madman!'

Yaye Khuredia frowned, and looked towards the men, who were returning from the cemetery.

The men had returned from the burial. Gnagna Guisse, the Thiandum family griot, welcomed them. The men stood apart, silent, their eyes lowered. They did not talk. A restrained hostility hung over the gloomy atmosphere. After a while, they withdrew, leaving a void in the Ndiobene concession.

Then it was the women's turn. The Ndiobene did not have a lively funeral wake as is the custom among us during that season.

At midday, the shining top of Guibril Guedj Diob's sunshade could be seen above the palisades, returning from the cemetery.

Neither that morning, nor after the tisbar prayer was there any talk, no game of yothe.

In his hut, Guibril Guedj Diob sat on a sheepskin, reading the Koran. Since the ban had been placed on him, he had lived alone like this. Even that morning, among his equals, there had been no exchange of courtesies.

Under the beintan tree, Dethye Law saw Medoune Diob in the company of his nephew, Tanor Ngone Diob. Then the ex-soldier entered the Ndiobene concession alone. A little later, his uncle went off in the direction of the niaye, carefully looking around him. He felt the eyes of the shoemaker on his back, and turned to look at him before continuing on his way.

Tanor Ngone Diob had slipped into the hut, and stood watching his father. In his eyes shone the narrow gleam of madness. His arms hung down by his sides. His thumb, guided by some obscure instinct, mechanically stroked the handle of his knife.

'How are you, son?' began Guibril Guedj Diob, by way of greeting.

A ray of light fell from the roof onto the back of his hand. His slender index finger held back the page. The amethyst beads of his rosary glittered. Tanor did not reply.

Guibril Guedj Diob closed the Book and made a quarter turn, pivoting round on his buttocks. The light made a white stripe on the back of his neck.

'Mother is dead,' said Tanor, in a tone which was neither interrogatory nor affirmative.

'Yes, son. Yallah has called her to his side.'

'What did she die of?'

Guibril Guedj Diob bowed his head reflectively, raising his forehead. His face was buried in the shadow.

'Yallah alone knows, son.'

'Perhaps she was sick?'

'That may be so, son. You may be right,' said his father.

His voice trembled. The ray of light had moved to the top of his head. His frizzy white hair glittered here and there. He went on, his voice thick with humility:

'That is so, son. That is so. You may be right. Sit down.'

He pointed with his hand to a place next to him.

'No!' thundered Tanor.

They fell silent. Time hung heavily.

'Mother is dead,' reiterated Tanor.

'Yes, son. Yallah has called her to his side.'

'What did she die of?'

'Yallah alone knows, son.'

'I have looked for Khar and cannot find her.'

'She must be in the house, son.'

'No, she is not in the house…'

'Perhaps you did not look properly.'

Once again, there was a silence. This time, in a voice of supplication, it was Guibril Guedj Diob who broke it.

'Stay in the house. You know the toubab-commandant is coming and I have to welcome him. No one but I can and ought to welcome him. One day you will take my place as chief. You have been to war. Since your return, we haven't spoken as father and son. I have things to confide to you.'

He waited in vain for a reply. Instead, like the first drops of rain on a zinc roof before a feverish storm, a mad laugh rose and filled the hut. Frightened, Guibril Guedj Diob invoked Yallah to himself.

'Where is Khar?' Tanor asked, after his burst of laughter.

'I repeat, in the house, son. Look carefully. Indeed, I want her myself. Go and fetch her for me.'

'No! She is not in the house. You are lying.'

Guibril Guedj Diob's arm twitched. His head moved. The sun's silvery rays fell on his shoulders.

Tanor Ngone Diob barked out again:

'Get up.'

'Why, son?'

Tanor Ngone Diob scratched his unkempt hair. His forage cap fell off. He asked again:

'Where is Khar?'

'In the house, son.'

'Khar has a child?'

'Yes.'

'A boy or a girl?'

'Son, I do not know. I heard a baby crying during the night.'

'It's not true,' yelled Tanor, drawing his knife.

'What isn't true, son?'

'Khar does not have a child. She is not married. I want to know where my mother is.'

The father had never doubted his son was mad. But he kept calm.

'I want to see my mother.'

'She is in the house, son.'

'Is that true?'

'Yes. It is true, son.'

'She isn't in her hut.'

'She can't be far. Perhaps she is with Khar, son.'

'Don't call me son. I am not your son.'

As he said this, Tanor advanced two paces towards his father. He went on:

'She doesn't love me.'

'Yes, she does love you. Khar also loves you. I think I heard their voices.'

Tanor listened. An innocent smile flitted across his face.

'I heard nothing,' he said.

'I did.'

'You want to chase me away?'

'No, son.'

'I am not your son,' snarled Tanor. 'Mother is dead. She said nothing to me. You are lying.'

This last rejoinder hurt the father's pride.

'I can hear her voice,' Tanor said.

'You can hear her voice? What did I say?'

'You are chasing me away?'

Suddenly, Tanor Ngone Diob began talking to himself. First, in French:

'Yes, Captain. No, Captain. The Vietcong are near the rice field. Your orders, Captain.' Then, in Wolof: 'Why do you want to go in there? Let them die. You won't get paid for it. Nor will your family. Take cover. Saw nothing! Understood, eh!'

Guibril Guedj Diob listened to his son. The son of whom he had been so proud. He had himself enlisted him for military service when the recruiting agents had come. After eight years' service, this son had returned to him from the paddy fields of Indochina and the jebels of North Africa, after spells in all the army mental homes.

The tacousan node sounded.

'Your mother is calling you, son.'

'You are sending me away.'

'No. It is true what I say. Come, it is time to pray. We will do it together, as before.'

'No. I don't pray.'

The tip of the knife came nearer. Guibril Guedj Diob raised his arm. Tanor, trained in hand to hand combat, flung him on the ground and, several times, the blade rose and fell.

IT IS SAID THAT THE BREEZE WHICH FROM TIME TO TIME caresses peoples' faces with its cool breath is the work of the women of Ouroulaïni, who live in Yallah's paradise, waiting to welcome the elect. So be it! The women of Ouroulaïni were at work, and a great many of them.

In the middle of the peinthieu, Tanor Ngone Diob performed his military manoeuvres, advancing, retreating, halting, all accompanied by a great deal of grimacing. He stood to attention, his hand at his temple, whistling the hymn to the dead.

'Ta a a tati tata a tati.'

The children surrounded him, imitating him. The dog watched them, lying on its side, covered with flies.

A man came out of the Ndiobene concession and headed almost at a run for the mosque. Removing his shoes at the entrance, he crossed the rows of faithful and spoke in the imam's ear. The latter, motionless, lips apart, blinked as if he had been struck dumb. Turning, he addressed the assembly:

'We are informed of the death of Guibril Guedj Diob. He has been killed by his son, Tanor Ngone Diob.'

All eyes turned to look at the middle of the peinthieu. Hurriedly, everyone left the mosque to meet at the Ndiobene concession, amid the weeping of the veudieu.

There were comments on all sides.

'I always said that Tanor Ngone Diob would kill one day. I even predicted it.'

'That is what he brought back for us from his wars.'

'All he did was learn to kill.'

'It's disturbing, all this,' said Semu.

'What is?' asked Palla.

'A mother who commits suicide, a son who kills his father, an incestuous daughter. Now there can be no doubt about Tanor Ngone Diob's madness.'

'It is the end of our village. Thank Yallah I am leaving soon,' said Amath.

'I am seriously thinking of leaving Santhiu-Niaye,' said Badieye.

'You, too?' asked Semu, lowering his voice.

'There is nothing more to be done at Santhiu-Niaye. Here come the women of Ouroulaïni. May Yallah let us enjoy their cool air.'

'Amine! Amine!' chorused the others.

The tree's shadow was lengthening towards the east. Three men, returning from the Ndiobene concession, seized Tanor Ngone Diob. They tied him to a large dead branch in the middle of the concession for all to see. Tanor Ngone Diob, immobilized though he was, continued to soliloquise about his wartime memories.

Dethye Law, assisted by Baye Yamar, prepared Guibril Guedj Diob's body for burial. Wrapped in a white shroud, like some inanimate object, it was carried away after the prayer for the dead by four of his peers, sticking out above the tops of the palisades. In front, Medoune Diob, carrying his elder brother's closed sunshade; next, the imam and Baye Yamar; and, following behind, the funeral cortège, chanting the hymn of the dead.

'*Allah! Allah!*'

'This is the first time in eight years that I have seen Guibril Guedj Diob without his sunshade,' said Palla to Badieye.

'Me, too. It was a present from Tanor Ngone Diob.'

'Medoune Diob has inherited it.'

'He will take everything. And he is now the village chief. Tomorrow he will welcome the toubab-commandant and the ten per cent tax.'

'You have understood, eh! We mustn't say anything about this affair to the toubab-commandant when he arrives. That is why he is being buried so quickly,' said Palla, and he intoned:

'*Allah! Allah!*'

The next day the toubab-commandant arrived, accompanied by his interpreter and two *gardes-cercle*. They were welcomed under the triumphal arch of palm fronds by Medoune Diob, the imam and Baye Yamar. Dethye Law had sent a message to say he was ill. Medoune Diob, richly dressed, carried the sunshade.

The toubab-commandant, the interpreter and the elders isolated themselves at the Ndiobene concession for discussions.

Questioned by the toubab-commandant, Medoune Diob replied:

'Guibril Guedj Diob is dead.'

The toubab-commandant replied:

'He was a good chief. And his son, Tanor?'

'He has gone to the town, like all the young men.'

A shadow of sorrow spread over the toubab-commandant's face. As he left, in front of everyone, he thanked the elders and praised the new chief they had chosen. Satisfied with his visit, the toubab-commandant then took his departure; the tax would be paid within three months.

Medoune Diob, as chief, had given his word.

———

TWO DAYS HAD PASSED. THEY WERE GATHERED, AS USUAL, under the tree: the imam, crosslegged, holding his beads and looking wise; Baye Yamar, more important than ever in his *tirailleur's* cap; Biram, with his boneless face. Medoune Diob lay on the couch, his arms crossed over the head-rest. In an affable, paternal tone of voice consonant with his position, he joined from time to time in the conversation.

A little to one side, the eternal game of yothe. Badieye and Gornaru, taciturn, indulged in their favourite pastime.

'Dethye Law, I hear you are leaving us today,' said Palla, watching the yothekat.

'Inchallah, Palla, I am leaving,' replied the griot-shoemaker, packing his things.

'May we know where you are going?'

Dethye Law straightened himself. He looked intently at the imam. The imam returned the craftsman's contemptuous gaze. Having decided, perhaps, that that was all the spiritual leader merited, Dethye Law bent over his packing.

Medoune Diob repeated the question:

'You haven't told us where you are going.'

Part of Medoune Diob's face showed above the head-rest.

'I am going where, I hope, the truth will be the concern of honest minds and not a privilege of birth,' rejoined Dethye Law.

'True, one must be a griot to possess that freedom.'

'Freedom of thought has never been a gift, nor an inheritance. It has always been bought for a heavy price in blood. The ruler who opposes it will find himself undone, sooner or later.'

'And is that freedom denied here?'

'No. In truth, no. It is early yet. But the basis of our community has been undermined. If it is not said now, it will be one day. You are not our chief. You are your brother's murderer, and our community has lost its foundation.'

'Take care what you are saying, Dethye Law,' interrupted Medoune Diob, abruptly getting up.

His eyes went from one elder to the next. Dethye Law continued:

'What have I said? People will not be able to say any more that truth is the weakness of Santhiu-Niaye.'

'My ancestors have always ruled Santhiu-Niaye, and yours have always served them.'

'That is indeed true. But that was in the past. I have inherited from my ancestors a concern for the truth which I shall preserve until the end.'

'Are you trying to say you are of noble blood?'

'Yes. The blood of truth is always noble, whatever its origin.'

'Yallah be praised that he is leaving. It is satan speaking in his mouth. Our village will be healthier without him,' said the imam.

'If a man loses the courage to proclaim the truth, he may as well die. I beg you, don't allow him to speak at our gatherings. He is not worthy of his role. He knows that Medoune Diob is the instigator of his elder brother's murder.'

Nervously, the imam tightened his fingers on his bead. Medoune Diob had sat down again.

His possessions packed, Dethye Law carried them on his head towards his house. He was joined by Palla, Badieye and Gornaru. After a few paces, they stopped. No one spoke. Gornaru broke the silence:

'Without you, the place will be empty. You have never approved when others have left. Why are you leaving now? Do you think you have been hurt more than we have? Your node is part of Santhiu-Niaye.'

'I leave reluctantly, Gornaru. Like anyone else, I am afraid of the unknown. I have a great respect for my role. Griot is not a synonym for servitude. You are high-born, but there are some things one must not accept, even if it places one's own life and the lives of one's family in danger.'

'Thank you for your advice,' said Badieye. 'I can see what you are getting at. You have always said out loud what others think to themselves, or merely murmur. But you are running away. If you cannot proclaim the truth where you were born, where you are one with the people around you, where will you be able to do so? Elsewhere? Elsewhere you will be a stranger. He who lets a small truth pass without proclaiming it will not stand up for the truth that places his life in danger.'

'You do not have to be a griot to proclaim the truth. There will always be someone who will be willing to do it. I ... I am afraid.'

'The moral courage to proclaim the truth was, yesterday, the privilege of the griot.'

'You talk about before ...'

'May Yallah keep you, Dethye Law!' said Badieye, going away.

'Amine! May Yallah help you, too.'

'Will you sing the node for us this tisbar?' asked Palla.

'Never again. That man over there is my imam no more. I prefer to pray outside the village.'

Saying this, Dethye Law continued on his way and went into his concession.

When Dethye Law came out again, preceded by his wife, Gnagna Guisse, and his children, it was after the ndjiolor. In the peinthieu, only the couch remained. The dog was chasing the flies. They crossed the square in single file and approached the entrance of the village in the direction of the setting sun, beneath its shower of mercury.

Once outside the village, Dethye Law told his wife to wait for him under the palm trees, while he climbed the sand dune. From there he could see the rooftops. He measured the time: it was time to call the faithful to prayer. He cupped his hands and sang his node.

The wind was blowing towards Santhiu-Niaye, so everyone heard the node. In ones and twos they converged on the peinthieu. Badieye, Palla, Gornaru and Semu, deep in conversation, arrived in front of the mosque. The imam, bent forward, was sitting in his place. Medoune Diob left his sunshade at the entrance, with his slippers.

Gornaru looked inquiringly about him, hesitant. Then, suddenly, Palla, who was standing on his own to one side, raised his hand to the level of his temple and began the prayer:

'Allahou ackbar!'

In silence, the others went and stood behind him. Dumbfounded, the imam straightened himself and looked at them, then looked behind himself, where he saw only Medoune Diob and Baye Yamar. Seeing Massar join the others, the imam bowed his head.

Medoune Diob, too, had seen. His gaze went from the imam to the others. He did not know what to do. When the others had finished the prayer, they shook hands with greater insistence than their faith required. Then the imam went out, without having prayed, leaving Medoune Diob alone.

Outside, they saw Dethye Law with his family. That evening, at the assembly, when they claimed he had run away, the griot replied:

'No, I didn't. I wanted to find out if there were still any men of worth in Senegal. For I know that if only once a man refuses to give witness to the truth in his own country, he may not travel. For the stranger has only his country for moral garb.'

It was also decided at this meeting that, now that Medoune Diob had been excluded, Khar Madiagua Diob must be driven from the village.

Early in the morning, Gnagna Guisse and Khar Madiagua Diob went out of Santhiu-Niaye. They left their footprints on the dew-covered ground as they followed the path that climbed, descended and wound around the sand dunes. They did not speak. Gnagna Guisse walked in front. Khar Madiagua Diob, a bundle on her head and the baby in her arms, followed behind.

The sun rose above the rim of the horizon. The clump of palm trees projected its tangled foliage over the glassy surface of the lake.

'We have arrived. Here we must part. You go straight on.

When you reach the seashore, go to the left. You won't meet anyone from Santhiu-Niaye.'

Khar Madiagua Diob nodded agreement.

'What sort of life will you have now? Only Yallah knows. Wherever you go now, no one will know and no one must know. Avoid talking about certain things. You know what you are leaving behind you. Before you, what will happen and what must happen isn't clear. Only Yallah knows. But your life will be what you make of it. Remember, wherever you go you will be among people. If you are a real descendant of the Thiandum-Thiandum, you will not be able to live chewing all the time over your resentment. You would poison your life and the lives of the people around you. Don't forget: a man only has himself as his remedy.'

After a pause, Gnagna Guisse went on:

'You are an orphan now. Therefore, an adult, and a mother. If, as you have told me, you are your father's victim, it still remains that you are a mother. This box I give to you now contains all the gold of the Thiandum. Your mother inherited it from her mother on her wedding day. She had built all her hopes on it. She had expected to be able to pass it on to you just as she received it on the day of her marriage. Yallah did not want it to be. You do not inherit the gold. It is for your daughter, Vehi-Ciosane Ngone Thiandum. May Yallah protect you.'

'I accept his protection.'

'Go! May Yallah watch over both of you.'

Gnagna Guisse stayed where she was until Khar Madiagua Diob was out of sight, murmuring:

'May Yallah ensure that, although that child is not of noble birth, it may acquire nobility and nobility of conduct. Out of them, the future will be born.'

The griot recalled the recent events. She would never have believed such a tale, or the rapidity with which it had all occurred, if she had had it from someone else. In the middle of the night, when the girl had given birth to her child, she had gone to her guelewar's hut. She found Ngone War Thiandum inert, the spider and the piece of poisonous root from the niaye in her hand. She approached her holding the petrol lamp, which was still alight. Her guelewar's mouth was open, flecked with a greenish foam. She wiped her lips, disposed of the spider and the root, before informing the Ndiobene and the elders of Santhiu-Niaye of her discovery.

Holding her baby, Khar Madiagua Diob walked on. The dunes followed one another; some were high, some were low. The sun had long since risen from the waters of the dawn and had deprived the last crests of their shade. Now it stood high in the sky. All morning, Khar Madiagua Diob had struggled against the morbid idea that had come into her head, trying to convince herself of its wrongfulness.

Finally, she let herself fall onto the ground under a sump tree, after clearing away the thorns lying about. She was obsessed with the thought of abandoning Vehi-Ciosane Ngone Thiandum. She sat with her legs folded, like at a family meal, breathing heavily. Her blood ran cold through her body. Tears spilled over her eyelids. Through the veil of tears, the vastness of the niaye opened out before her. Fear? Hysteria? Anger? She was agitated, and her whole body trembled. Biting her lip, she raised her narrow forehead, obstinately, towards the gaps in the thin leaves. With a forced, yet maternal gesture, she drew the child onto her lap and changed it.

She waited under the sump tree for the sun to lose its strength. Feeling rested, she set off again, chewing all the time over her anger. She spent the night among some trees, sleeping fitfully. Myriads of stars shone in the sky.

The next day, she set off again with the baby in her arms. The thought of abandoning Vehi-Ciosane took hold of her. As she walked, the smell of seaweed became more persistent and hung tenaciously about her. A haze stretched across the horizon. From the top of the fourth dune, she saw the dark green expanse, which shimmered in the middle like a piece of corrugated iron. She descended the slope. She went to the water's edge. She walked barefoot along the beach, enjoying the pleasantly warm feeling of

the water. Laughing, frilly waves came tumbling towards her.
The water covered her ankles now. Khar Madiagua Diob looked
about her. Not a soul in sight. She stopped, hesitating. Fear?
Remorse? Cowardice? Selfishness? She bit her lip, undecided.
The child in her arms was crying. She let it cry. Its cries spread
out across the sea. Like the bells at dawn, they reverberated
through her head.

She returned to the shore, fed the baby, and set off towards the
left. From behind, the sun beat down on both of them. It was
easier walking on the sand of the beach. She forced herself to
walk faster. She had begun to tremble again. After four hours,
her legs were overcome with weariness. Tenaciously, she pressed
on. Long past the place where she had turned, she saw a black
speck. Alert, she increased her pace and hurried towards the speck,
hoping it would be people. At a distance of two hundred yards,
she made out two men loading a lorry with sand. Coming up to
them, she greeted them. They returned her greeting.

'Woman, where do you come from?' she heard herself being
asked by a third man. He was holding something—she could not
make out what it was—in his hand.

'Who? Me?'

'Yes, you, woman,' said the man, a little younger than the
other two, his canvas shirt hanging outside his European trousers.

'From over there,' she replied, pointing to the niaye.

The two workmen, who had stopped what they were doing,
looked at her in surprise.

'Where are you going,' the third man asked again.

'I want to go to Ndakaru.'

'Ndakaru?' repeated the man, astonished.

She did not reply. She held her bundle on her head. The man's
curiosity made her wary.

'We aren't going to Ndakaru,' said the man, hoisting himself
up onto the side of the lorry and busying himself inside. He went
on: 'Ndakaru is far. I can put you down at the crossroads. There
you will find another lorry to take you to Ndakaru. How much
have you got?'

'Nothing.'

'Nothing? You can't get to Ndakaru with nothing.'

With this, the driver lost interest in her.

She stood where she was, glancing sideways at him.

With a regular rhythm, the spadefuls of sand fell into the lorry. Soon, the strong masculine voice of one of the two men let out a *Djinah O*.

'Come round this side. It is getting hot,' the driver said to her.

She obeyed, and settled herself down in the shade of the lorry. The falling of the sand woke the baby, and it began to cry. She placed it on her lap and from the opening of her blouse took out a breast. The crying stopped.

'It's a fresh new baby,' said the driver, stating a fact.

'Yes.'

'You are going to Ndakaru to look for work?'

'Yes.'

'It's a bit late in the season. I've heard it's hard for mothers to find work as maids.'

'I have relatives there.'

Without realizing what she was doing, her knee kept time with her song as she rocked Vehi-Ciosane. Like waves of pleasure splashing her face, marked by her labour and the fatigue of walking, thin streams of light crossed her eyes.

'Finished, boss,' announced one of the men.

'Let's go, then. Abdou, you go behind. You, get in here with me.'

'Right, boss,' said Abdou.

In the cabin, the driver asked her:

'A girl or a boy?'

'A girl.'

'Pity. What name?'

'Vehi-Ciosane Ngone Thiandum.'

'I have never heard such a name: Vehi-Ciosane ... Which Thiandum was her father?'

Khar Madiagua, gently, held her baby tight, pulled her bundle under her feet, and looked in front of her. The man watched her, sideways, then started the engine without getting an answer.

With the immensity of the niaye on one side and the immensity of the sea on the other, the lorry drove off, leaving behind it the double track made by its wheels, which the sea came to lick. This story had no other ending: it was a page in their life. A new one starts, which depends on them.

And if, one day, you should happen to go into the niaye and to the village of Santhiu-Niaye, don't ask them any questions. Of me, perhaps they will say: he came once.

The one visit was enough.

Ndakaru, Gamu 1965

THE MONEY-ORDER

HIS BODY WAS RUNNING WITH SWEAT. HIS SHIRT CLUNG TO his skin. His face was shining. Breathing heavily, his mouth open, the postman struggled through the sand with his bicycle. Gripping the handlebars firmly, chest forward, he climbed the sandhill, cursing the inhabitants and the authorities.

'What are they waiting for to get the road tarred?' he thought.

Housewives returning from the market called out to him in fun:

'Eye! man, you've wet yourself!'

They left him behind. He stopped. Resting his bicycle against his belly, which stuck out suggestively, he wiped his face with his cotton handkerchief. He kept his eyes on the women's backs; nimble and light, their calebashes balanced on their heads, they hardly seemed to touch the ground.

He set off again at a slower pace.

The houses were nearly all identical: built of old, rotten wood, with roofs of corrugated iron, which was invariably rusty, or of old thatch that had never been renewed, or even of black oilcloth.

The postman stood his bicycle against the twisted stake of the doorway. Two women were seated on the ground. They returned his greeting with suspicion. They knew him, but because of his job, the man carried with him an unfavourable prejudice.

'Women, is your husband, Ibrahima Dieng, at home?'

Mety, the elder of the two women, and the first wife, looked up inquiringly into the man's face and then at his hands.

'Who, you say?'

'Mety,' interpolated the postman, 'Mety, I live in this quarter myself and I know that Ibrahima Dieng is the master of this house. I am not a toubab.'

'Bah *(the postman's name)*, what have I said?'

'Nothing, in fact. Nothing that could send you to hell.'

'You know very well that our man is never at home at this time of day. Idle, yes. But wallow all day among our skirts, that, no! You ask as if you were a stranger.'

'I must do my work. When you see me, you women all act as if you'd seen an alcati (policeman).'

'You are worse than an alcati. You only have to leave a paper once or twice for the tax men to come and carry off our things. You have never brought good news to this house.'

'Just so. This morning it's the opposite.'

'Ah!' said Mety, quickly getting to her feet. Her dress hung from her prominent behind.

'Harpy! as soon as money's mentioned, there you are, wriggling like worms. It's money.'

'Where from?'

'From Paris. A money-order.'

'Paris? Who does Ibrahima know in Paris? Are you sure it is for him? Bah, don't kill us with hope.'

'There is even a letter with it. I know my job.'

'You heard, Aram,' called Mety, happily, to the second wife, who had come up to them. She was younger, thin and hollow-cheeked, with a pointed chin.

'A money-order for how much?' asked Aram.

'Twenty-five thousand francs[1].'

They marvelled at the amount.

'Yallah has come to us at last, Mety. And you were always going on about our bad luck!' said Aram.

Mety held the advice-note and the letter in her hand. It gave her a delightful feeling of power, of wealth.

'A letter and a money-order! Who can have sent them?'

'A toubab. In Paris there are only toubabs! Mety, do you think our man tells us everything?'

'Shall we give the letter to Bah?'

'No, women, no. It isn't my job to read or write letters.' With that, the postman left them.

During the previous night they had both been kept awake by the same problem. In their minds, they had gone the rounds of all the shopkeepers in the quarter. They owed money to all of them.

'We can't wait for our man to get back to find out what we will eat this midday. I'm sure that Mbarka will advance us a kilo of rice and half a litre of oil on the strength of this advice-note and the letter. There is still a little dried fish and nyebe left over from

---

[1] Equivalent to 500 French francs, or about £40 sterling (Translator).

yesterday.'

'That is what we must do,' agreed Aram, after a moment's reflection.

Together they set off, each holding a child by the hand.

He had not asked where the rice had come from, so well seasoned with dried fish and nyebe. He had eaten his fill; it had been a real blow-out. He gave two magnificent belches and said, 'Allahou ackbar'. He was sitting on his sheepskin, at the foot of the bed.

'Is there a little kola left,' he asked, without addressing either of his wives directly.

'Look in the jar next to the drinking water,' called his second wife, from outside.

'Aram, these aren't left-overs!' he called out to his wives, as he made his choice. 'Four nuts of every shade! You aren't going to tell me that Yallah made it rain pocket-books full of money this morning or that one of you has inherited from old Lebu!'

'No, Dieng! Yallah, in his infinite goodness, never abandons his faithful.'

'Indeed, wives! Indeed, allahou ackbar! In his greatness, his goodness is immeasurable. He helps us day and night.'

'Wait ... wait, before you break the nut and share it out.' Mety entered and placed in front of him on the sheepskin a small bowl containing slices of juicy pawpaw swimming in a little sugared water.

'My favourite fruit! Wash the kola for me.' She went out again.

He bit into the soft flesh of the pawpaw. It melted in his mouth and the juice trickled over his lips.

'Bring me something to wipe myself.'

'Straight away, Dieng.'

Aram brought a piece of old cloth and sat down next to him. She busied herself tidying up. Dieng washed his hands again. Mety came back and he chose a quarter of kola from her palm.

He got up with difficulty and lay down on the bed, reciting verses from the Koran.

'I wonder if I'll have the strength to go to the mosque?' he said to himself.

'There is an old beggar,' announced Aram.

Before answering her, he found a comfortable position and stretched out his legs. His wives and children were forbidden to give alms to able-bodied men or to young men. These two categories were parasites, he said, on the look-out for a free meal. When this was discussed at the mosque among the heads of families, he gave no quarter, relentlessly countering the arguments of his critics and demanding proof from the suras that the faithful had to give alms to these people.

'He is really an old man?' he asked.

'Yes.'

'All right, then. Give him the left-overs. And may Yallah make all our misfortunes follow them.'

This was his ritual form of words whenever he gave alms.

Every now and then, a cool wind made the curtains billow. According to popular belief, blessed wives living in paradise were fanning themselves. Dieng lay stretched out. He took a deep breath and yawned.

'Excuse me, Mety. Rub my legs for me. How I have walked today!'

'You musn't complain. Yallah is great. He will never abandon us.'

'Yallah! Yallah! One must cultivate one's field.'

Obediently, Mety rubbed each of his legs in turn, up to his back. Dieng was soon asleep. She crept out on tip-toe.

'Did you tell him?' asked Aram, when Mety returned to her place on the mat.

'Not yet. Let him rest. When the muezzin calls, I'll wake him and tell him,' replied Mety, looking round for a place to lie down.

Thanks to the stifling midday heat, they were soon asleep.

He had woken up, after the time for prayer. He emptied his anger onto Aram and Mety, speaking out loud to himself.

'Seems as if I live in a house of unbelievers and infidels. I wonder if you ever pray, either of you, when I'm not here. And I begin to wonder, too, about the faith of my children.'

Neither replied. After he had washed, as a good believer and master of his wives, he guided them along the path of Yallah. The two women stood a few paces behind him, imitating his gestures.

The prayers over, he was about to go out when Mety, like an old cat stretching its paws, said:

'Nidiaye, dear, Bah the postman came. You have a letter.'

'A letter? Who from? What colour is the paper?'

'No, it isn't a paper for the tax.'

'What do you know about it?'

'Bah told us it has come from Paris. The money-order as well.'

'Money-order?'

'Yes.'

'Who has sent me a money-order?'

'Your nephew, Abdou. He is in Paris.'

'Listen, let's go into the house. We can't talk about money in the street.'

Inside, Mety continued:

'Abdou has sent you 25,000 francs. There are 2,000 for you and 3,000 for his mother. The remaining 20,000 francs he wants you to keep for him. He greets you. He asks you to reply when you receive his letter and the money-order.'

'I hope the whole quarter doesn't know about the money-order.'

'Well … I went with Aram to Mbarka's shop. Mbaye was there, and he read me the letter.'

'So Mbarka knows about it.'

Dieng raised his chin angrily.

'You should not have had the letter read to you, nor obtained credit from that robber Mbarka without asking me first.'

'There was nothing to eat for today.'

'Nor yesterday,' added Aram. 'We can't keep the children alive without feeding them. The children can't live on hunger.'

'A good wife waits to be told *(this was said in French)*. Now the whole quarter will know that I've had a money-order.'

They bore the heat of their man's anger in silence. He told them off roundly. Then, with the letter and the advice-note in his pocket, he left the house with a lordly step, his head high.

Dieng had a weakness for clothes. The silk embroidery around the neck of his large boubou had been done by hand in a variety of motifs in a blend of white, yellow and violet threads. This desire to impress his neighbour, this taste for clothes, always raised him a degree above the person to whom he was talking, whose only worth, in his eyes, lay in his appearance and his dress.

Mbarka's shop stood on the corner of the two streets. It was lopsided. It was shabby on the outside, and the inside was hardly any better. The merchandise was crammed onto rickety shelves held up by wire and strips of leather. In the evening, clusters of flies took up residence. The counter, made of unpolished wood, was thick with dust.

When Dieng entered the shop, the two men exchanged a polite flow of salamalecs.

'Mety came in earlier to buy some things. Did I do right in letting her have them?' asked the shopkeeper.

'You did right. In fact I have just received a small money-order which will enable me to pay my account,' said Dieng, sourly. 'Can you tell me how much I owe you?'

'May Yallah forgive me and forgive all believers the thought you seem to attribute to me. Perhaps I didn't hear properly … Between neighbours, I think it is preferable to talk things over before they come to the ears of strangers. Why do you ask me for your account? It isn't because of that money-order, I hope! I only asked Mety to get you to call because I have received some rice. New, coarse-grained rice.'

With eyes bulging and eyelashes bristling, the shopkeeper looked first to the left and then to the right. He leant over to Dieng and carefully unfolded a square piece of red cloth in which lay a few fine, fat grains of rice. In a low, expressionless voice, he went on:

'It's rice from Indochina. Not American rice, or French rice. This rice is more economical than all the others. I only have enough for my special customers, like you.'

Mbarka wrinkled his forehead, his watery sheep's eyes sparkled.

Dieng was not enthusiastic, but he was anxious to keep the advantage, so he touched the rice with the tips of his fingers. Like an electric shock, a shudder ran through him, right to the extremeties of his hair. Mbarka scrutinized his customer's face.

'This is the rice you ate today. What do you think of it? It is easy to digest. It doesn't stick together when you cook it, like toubab rice. It isn't starchy. Look at its surface, so natural! What do you think? I'll put fifteen kilos aside for you. I can't spare any more than that,' he concluded, re-folding his piece of cloth.

'How much is it a kilo?'

'The same price. Yallah is my witness, I had to grease a lot of palms to get this rice. What quality! And who for? For you, my friends. Do you think I want to make money out of you? If I told you how many people owed me money, you'd soon see how little profit I make. I merely believe I ought to get my money back. I'd rather lose my profit on the fifteen kilos of rice than lose your esteem.'

Mbarka had convinced Dieng. As for his account, he need only call in on his way back from the post-office. To prove his friendship, Mbarka broke a kola nut with him, saying, half jokingly, half seriously:

'Collect your rice soon, or I'll give it to someone else who can pay cash.'

Dieng did not wait to be told twice. He called out to a little boy who was passing:

'Fetch your mother Mety.'

Still without losing his advantage, he borrowed fifty francs from Mbarka to pay his fare.

Barely across the road after leaving Mbarka's shop, Dieng was stopped by his neighbour, Gorgui Maïssa, an incurable borrower and a rogue.

'Ibrahima ... Dieng!'

'Maïssa ...Fall! How are you?'

'Alhamdoulillah! ... And your family?'

'The same, alhamdoulillah!'

Gorgui Maïssa's head was round, in spite of his handwoven

cotton cap and his prominent forehead. His caftan fluttered in the breeze.

A few yards ahead, Bah the postman appeared over the rise, pushing his bicycle, his shirt unbuttoned; he wore nothing underneath. His stomach, bulging out around his waist, hung down over his knees. After the customary greetings, they walked side by side.

'You've seen the letter and the ...'

The postman did not finish. A look from Dieng reminded him that 'you don't talk about money in the street'. All the same, Dieng acknowledged the question with a grunt.

'News from where?'

'A nephew.'

'It is always a pleasure to know that the young are thinking of us. It's their duty to look after those who are older than they are. Alas, my nephews ignore me. I receive nothing from anyone,' added Gorgui Maïssa.

'What do you expect? Things are given to me and I deliver them. I am everyone's messenger,' said Bah, feeling that he was being got at.

'I wasn't referring to you.'

'I'm a bit behind. See you later at the mosque,' said Bah, climbing onto his bicycle.

Dieng was not pleased with Gorgui Maïssa's company. 'Does he know that I am going to the post-office? How could he not know? Mbarka's shop is a public place. Nothing is secret there.'

'Did you know Mbarka has got some very good rice in? From Indochina.'

'No,' replied Dieng.

'What? That's why I didn't come and disturb the two of you. Mbarka likes secrets that aren't.'

'I went to the shop to check my account,' said Dieng, in his most natural tone of voice. 'He is going to think I have some money. Where is he going, anyway?' he reflected.

'I'm telling you, then. He refused to give me credit. But you go and see him when we get back. He is selling it under the counter. He's a crook, that Mbarka. You owe him a hundred francs, you've only gone two steps and it's doubled. He would suck the bones of a hundred-year-old corpse!'

They fell into conversation. Both admitted they only managed to feed their families by living on credit. Prices had gone up so much.

'This world is a bitter place for us,' sighed Gorgui Maïssa.

When they reached the bus-stop, Dieng asked:

'Where are you going, Maïssa?'

'I'm going with you,' he replied, pulling himself onto the bus in front of Dieng.

———

THE INTENSE HEAT MINGLED WITH THE SUFFOCATING smell of exhaust fumes that fouled the air. The square swarmed with cripples, lepers and ragged children, all of them lost in that ocean. Drinking water overflowed from one basin into the cleaner one beneath it. Carts grated on their axles, cars and motor-cycles made a deafening din. A cunning old beggar held out his hand with its five fingers wasted by leprosy to the occupants of cars brought to a stop by the traffic lights. A blind woman, the mother of a little girl, lay stretched out in the road itself, calling in a barely audible falsetto voice.

Dieng and Gorgui Maïssa entered the post-office together. There were people waiting at all the windows. Gorgui Maissa made inquiries and led Dieng to the window marked MONEY-ORDERS. There was a long queue here as well, with a fat old woman at the end of it. Probably because she was tired and at the end of her patience, she had sat down on the floor, indifferent to all that was going on around her. She looked like a shapeless stump of flesh, so completely had her features disappeared.

Leaning against the counter, Gorgui Maïssa, his face close-up, watched the clerk counting the notes.

The time passed.

'Keep my place. I'm going to find someone to read me my letter.'

Dieng found the letter-writer installed next to the post-box. He was about to refuse the letter, but Dieng explained that his wife had opened it thinking it was for herself. The letter-writer had a nose like an elephant's foot, and wore steel-rimmed spectacles that kept slipping down his nose. He looked at Dieng over the top of his spectacles, making him feel awkward.

'The letter comes from Paris. It is from your nephew, Abdou.' He read:

Paris.
19 *July* 196...

Dear Uncle,
I am writing to ask you for news of yourself. How are you and your family? As for me, God be thanked, all is well. I wish and pray God that it is the same with all of you. I am profiting from the visit of my friend, Diallo, to write to you.

As you have probably learned, I am in Paris. God be thanked, I am well. I think of you day and night. I have not come to France to play the beggar or the bandit, but to find work and earn a little money and, God willing, to learn a good trade. There is no work in Dakar. I couldn't spend my time all day, year in and year out, sitting doing nothing. *When you are young, that is not good. I borrowed money to come here. It is true I never said anything to you or to my mother about my thoughts. I couldn't stay there just watching and living on the air of time. I am old enough now to* marry, *to have my own wife. I have repaid the money I borrowed. That is why I have never written or sent anyone any money since I arrived in France. God be thanked, my way is now clear. You mustn't listen to what you hear. If you are a* failure *in France, it is because you want to be one. After work, I come home and say my five prayers. If it pleases God and his prophet Mohammed, a drop of alcohol will never pass my lips. I am sending you this money-order for* 25,000 *CFA francs. Keep* 20,000 *francs for me. Give* 3,000 *francs to my mother and take* 2,000 *francs for yourself. I know you don't always have work. I have written to my mother. Tell her I am well.*

I greet aunt Mety, aunt Aram and the children. Next time, I will send

*the children something. Keep the money for me. If it pleases God, I shall
return home. Do not forget me in your prayers.*

*I greet you.
Your nephew,*
ABDOU.

The letter-writer translated into Wolof as he read. A beggar with
watery eyes came up, led by a child, repeating all the time,
'Ngir Yallah, by the grace of God.'

The letter-writer handed the letter back and said:

'Fifty francs.'

Dieng hunted. He had only ten francs left. His fare, along with
Gorgui Maïssa's, had reduced what money he had by forty francs.

'I'll cash my money-order and come back and pay you.'

'What do you think I live on?' asked the letter-writer. He eyed
his customer with suspicion.

Dieng held out the advice-note for him to see.

'All right, I'll wait,' he said, convinced.

The fat woman had left, muttering about wasting her time,
even though she had got what she had come for. Dieng went up to
the window. The post-office clerk extracted a slip and compared
it with the advice-note.

'Ibrahima Dieng, your identity card.'

'Man, I haven't got an identity card. I have my tax receipt and
my voter's card.'

'Is there a photo?'

'No … No.'

'Give me something with a photo on it. Driving licence, military
service certificate.'

'I have nothing like that.'

'Well, go and get an identity card, then.'

'Where from?'

All that could be seen above the window was an oval black ball,
out of all proportion with the tubercular shoulders upon which
it rested. At the question, 'Where from?', the clerk looked up at

Dieng. It was a closed face. From the neck upwards, it was all severity. Dieng was cowed.

'I've got an identity card,' intervened Gorgui Maïssa, stretching his arm out with his card held between thumb and index finger, and looking at the clerk.

'Is the money-order in your name?'

Gorgui Maïssa did not reply. He held his arm out for a few seconds, then withdrew it.

'Get away from here,' thundered the clerk.

'Ibrahima Dieng, are you going to give me your identity card or not?'

'Man, I have no card,' Dieng replied in a quavering voice.

'Go and get one.'

'Where from?'

They looked at each other. Dieng thought he saw a look of contempt appear in the civil servant's eyes. He suffered. He came out in a cold sweat of humiliation. He felt as if a painful bite had been taken out of his flesh. He said nothing. There came into his mind the saying that circulated among all the ordinary people of Dakar: 'Never upset a civil servant. He has great power.'

'Go and ask the police in your quarter,' advised the clerk at last, returning Dieng's advice-note. 'The money-order will remain here for two weeks.'

Gorgui Maïssa and Dieng hung around the window for a while.

On their way out: 'Is that the way you pay me?'

It was the letter-writer, who grabbed Dieng by the scruff of his neck.

'What?'

'What? ... My work!'

'Ask your due without shouting or rumpling my clothes,' said Dieng, removing the letter-writer's hands from his boubou.

'Man, we haven't cashed the money-order yet. He hasn't got an identity card,' said Gorgui Maïssa, intervening in an effort to calm the scribe.

'That's not my concern.'

'Don't shout,' interrupted Dieng, haughtily. 'Yallah knows I haven't got fifty francs. I am going to the police. I'll come back and pay you. I never use other people's property. I am a believer.'

'A believer? A crook, more like it. Go and find work instead of pretending to be a marabout,' sneered the letter-writer, going back to his place.

What was happening? Dieng did not know, but as he went down the stairs, he felt humiliated. In front of the post-office, the beggars, ranged like pots of faded flowers, held out their hands and their begging bowls, crying their woes. Dieng re-arranged his clothes, asking Gorgui Maïssa to see if they were rumpled or dirty behind.

'If we go to the police station, will we have time to come back for the money-order?'

Gorgui Maïssa examined the sky, the shadow thrown by the plane-trees and his pocket-watch.

'It is possible.'

'I mean on foot.'

'That changes everything.'

Although Maïssa's presence gave him moral support, he was thinking of his fifty francs. Had he been on his own, he would have been able to go there and back by bus.

'Are you coming with me?'

'Yes,' replied Maïssa, surprised by the question.

'I'll make him walk fast. He is banking on the money-order. What bad luck!'

Gorgui Maïssa trotted behind. He had found out at the shop that Dieng had received a money-order. As he wanted to touch him for a loan, he was staying with him. He was banking on at least five thousand francs. On his way out, he had said to one of his wives:

'Wait for me. I'll be back with money for the day's expenses.'

Exhausted and sweating, they crossed the courtyard of the police-station. Gorgui Maïssa promptly slumped down onto the steps that encircled the building: an old villa in the colonial style turned over to the use of the police. Here and there, groups of people sat on the steps talking. Near a door two policemen in untidy uniforms sat with their legs sprawled out in front of them. In a weary voice, one of them indicated the way:

'Identity cards? Over there ...'

Dieng entered a corridor.

'Eye! Where are you going?'

Startled, he jumped. The voice had nothing normal or human about it. Dieng turned round. Nothing. Warily he advanced a few paces.

'Eye! It's you I'm talking to. Where are you going?'

The cavernous voice was clearly addressing itself to him. He started when a firm grip shook him roughly.

'Don't you know it is prohibited to enter here?'

A spasm of rage and repressed anger came over him, momen-. tarily paralysing his tongue and his reflexes. A sensation of thirst knotted his throat. He made a great effort to swallow his saliva. He saw the face, turned three-quarters towards him. It was a face carved in charred wood, badly finished, with thick lips.

'That man over there told me this was the way for identity cards,' he replied, in a voice which betrayed his nervousness.

'Get out!' bellowed the man. '*Aitia cibiti*.'

Out of countenance and biting his lower lip, Dieng replaced his elhadj cap and slowly withdrew, nervously smoothing his boubou as he went.

'Money for a kola nut,' Gorgui Maïssa greeted him.

Dieng looked him up and down with contempt, then handed him a coin. He joined the queue.

'We have time for the tacousan prayer,' Gorgui Maïssa said to him.

Maïssa acted as imam. He was quick. Dieng went back to his place in the queue, taking a quarter of kola with him. The queue made no progress. There were murmurs of discontent about the slowness of the service.

All of a sudden, Gorgui Maïssa's voice drowned the other noises. He had become a griot, extolling the noble lineage of a young man dressed in European clothes: the beauty of the women, the boundless generosity and bravery of the men, the nobility of their conduct, all of it redounding on the young man, pure blood, sang Gorgui Maïssa, from the purest of blood. And on he went, unflagging, from one theme to the next, in deep Wolof. He finally broke the young man's resistance, indifferent though he was to the traditional praises.

The crowd listened. The young man, visibly embarrassed, tried unsuccessfully to quieten this impromptu adulation.

'I don't sing for money. When one finds one's sanga (master) in such a place, it is right to make him known to the people of my station. I don't sing for money. I want to keep the tradition alive,' sang Maïssa.

Defeated, the young man slipped him a hundred-franc note. Maïssa's voice soared as the young man left.

'You know him?' Dieng asked, when calm had returned.

'Know him? You *are* simple. I heard someone mention his santa, his family name, and I embroidered on it.'

'As far as I could make out, you were getting the santas and lineages mixed up.'

'He didn't see that. He was happy to hear himself talked about. You know nothing about life today.'

'No,' admitted Dieng, overcome by Gorgui Maïssa's lack of dignity in pretending to be a griot.

'Neither does he. We are wasting our time here,' added Maïssa, his thoughts elsewhere.

Then came Dieng's turn.

Behind the window appeared an adolescent with close-cropped hair and sporting a pair of Lumumba glasses, which gave his juvenile's face the indefinable air of an intellectual.

'What can I do for you?'

'I want an identity card.'

'Birth certificate, three photos and a fifty-franc stamp.'

'Look, son,' explained Dieng, moving his head nearer, until the top of his cap pressed against the top of the window. 'I have a money-order to cash and if I don't have an identity card ...'

With these words, he produced the advice-note. The clerk took it from him. The glasses turned in his direction, far-off eyes fluttered their lids:

'It is true, but there is nothing I can do. Go and fetch your birth certificate, the photos and the stamp, old man,' he said in French, in an impersonal tone of voice.

'You want a piece of paper to prove who I am. I have my last tax receipt and my voter's card. Here ...'

'It is no use, old man,' he replied, pushing Dieng's hand away. Without photos, birth certificate and stamp, there is nothing I can do. Make way for the next person.'

Dieng straightened up. He felt dizzy. He looked around for Maïssa.

'Man, your friend has left. He said he had to go somewhere.'

'What?'

'He asked me to tell you.'

'Thank you, woman,' he said, going down the steps.

'A visit to the post-office and back isn't like climbing to the moon. Where is he? Instead of thinking of us and the children, he will be playing the generous rich man, and the money will flow from his hands like water through his fingers. Perhaps he's got his eye on a young girl! Some shameless hussy who will suck his money away like her mother's milk.'

All afternoon Mety's thoughts had run along these lines. Neighbours had sent their children once or twice to find out if Dieng was back. 'Parasites! As soon as they hear someone has money, there they are, like vultures.'

Dieng came home late. He had been to the mosque. The evening meal was the equal of the midday meal. The two wives anticipated his least wishes. After the kola nut, Mety, encouraged by the presence of her veudieu, ventured:

'How did you get on?'

'I have nothing,' he replied. 'I need an identity card. For that, I need a birth certificate, a fifty-franc stamp and three photos.'

They did not believe him. The two wives looked at one another.

Mety intended to pursue the matter further, but decided to wait for a more opportune moment. She told her husband that there were people to see him. She said how many.

'They are all going to believe that I have money and that I am refusing to help them. They can ask Gorgui Maïssa. He was with me ...'

'It was only to borrow money from you that he went with you, the old miser,' objected Aram, interrupting him.

Dieng told them how Maïssa had extracted a hundred francs from the credulous young man.

'He made himself scarce to avoid having to share it with you. Talk about mean! And you have spent your fifty francs. What times!'

A new arrival announced himself with a long litany of greetings. It was Madiagne Diagne. The women withdrew. The two men talked about one thing and another. The conversation was interspersed with periods of silence.

'I came to see you. I am faced with a serious, indeed a critical, situation and I have come to you for help.'

Madiagne Diagne paused. It was not easy to break the abcess. He must deploy his argument point by point. He must struggle, mortify himself by humiliating himself first of all for being in such need. His words must correspond with the expression on his face, his voice must be unctuous without any stress on the Wolof syllables. He must be ready to talk himself hoarse, giving his hearer time to be overcome, to be possessed by his misery. He must swear on the Koran and by Yallah, promise to pay by tomorrow before sunrise, knowing full well that tomorrow is not today's child.

Dieng half understood. For everyone, without exception, used the same approach. Firstly, appeal to your hearer's sense of solidarity with those in misery; by soft words, stir his feeling of fraternity, even though it evaporates from one day to the next. Dieng remained silent. Madiagne Diagne kept repeating, like a refrain, the arguments he had already used.

'Yallah is my witness, I have not cashed the money-order.

Perhaps tomorrow.'

'You don't need to swear, I believe you. I only need five thousand francs or whatever you can advance me. You are my last hope.'

'You can ask Gorgui Maïssa. He was with me,' repeated Dieng, sympathetic.

'Perhaps you can lend me three kilos of rice. I heard you had received a hundred kilos.'

'People talk too much and exaggerate. I only have fifteen kilos. Mety! Mety!'

'Dieng!'

'Give Madiagne three kilos of rice.'

'Nidiaye, we haven't much left.'

'Mety, don't argue! Whenever I tell you something, it's always the same.'

'It is for my family, Mety,' said Madiagne Diagne. 'I swear to you that the children haven't eaten all day.'

'Madiagne, you know that our house is yours. I don't hide anything from you. I'll go and see what we have left. As he said, he hasn't cashed the money-order.'

The men renewed the banalities of conversation, banalities of the kind that people familiar with one another repeat several times a day, and which they find useful, although they are nothing more than a way of filling in the emptiness of their boredom.

Madiagne Diagne left with half a kilo of rice.

Mety and her veudieu could not understand their husband. His generosity was stupid. The whole quarter would come flocking and they would be left with nothing. Food was the province of the women, and they intended to defend it. They put their heads together. They would be the ones to decide who should be helped. Although generations of docility had made the women of our part of the world obedient and submissive, they had learned in the process that they could get anything they wanted from the men.

Other heads of family came in their turn. In spite of their pleas, they left empty-handed.

Before sunrise the next day, Dieng went as usual to the mosque for the fadyar prayer. When he returned, the women had finished their household chores. He was drinking his quinqueliba tea, when Baïdy arrived. He was a walking skeleton, with very prominent features. He had not been able to come the day before. His presence this morning was of the utmost importance, he said, sharing Dieng's breakfast. Dieng did not let him finish. Full of regrets, he said, sadly:

'Yallah is my witness, I have received nothing.'

Mety, who was present at the discussion, put in:

'Baïdy, I was about to go round to you, hoping to find something.'

With his sculptured face, and his neck tensed with disappointment, Baïdy withdrew. Mety, pleased with her success, glanced knowingly at her veudieu.

From Dieng's house to the town hall was at least five kilometres. The thought of the distance appalled him. Go there on foot! If only he had twenty francs! Who could lend him the money? In his present situation, no one would help him. He thought of Gorgui Maïssa and his hundred francs of the day before. Maïssa's house was on the opposite side of the road of his despair. Recognizing Dieng's voice exchanging greetings with his wives, Maïssa came out to meet him. He drew Dieng out of the house and swore on the gods watching over him that he hadn't anything left. In fact, he said, he was about to call on Dieng. When Dieng told him he was going to the town hall, he excused himself on account of his rheumatism.

Dieng set off at a gentle pace on foot. Five kilometres or more!

The anonymous crowd flowed hurriedly in the same direction. The hooting of cars, the backfiring of motor-cycles, the ringing of bicycle bells, the flip-flop of worn-out shoes, the clip-clop of horses' hooves accompanied the crowd to the outskirts of what was known as the 'Native Quarter', where they split and went off in different directions. The noises gradually faded, but the veil of grey smoke still hung in the air.

Outside the main entrance of the town hall, and on the steps, swarms of people were gathered. Hands were being shaken all round. An aged orderly, enthroned like a king, held forth with gusto.

'Birth certificate? Registry office, over there,' he answered, in reply to Dieng's query, his arm outstretched to show the direction.

'Another queue,' thought Dieng, seeing how long it was. He stood at the end. Different accents and guttural tones hummed around him. He began talking to the person in front of him: a thin fellow, whose face was scarred with tribal markings. It was the third time he had come for the same thing. He was a bricklayer and had found a job in Mauretania. He had been out of work for two years. Dieng wanted to know how long it would take to get a birth certificate.

'That depends,' said the bricklayer,' on whether they know you or you have contacts. If you don't, all you can do is try not to get discouraged. But if you have money, well, then, things go quickly.'

Dieng confided in him. The bricklayer seemed to have experience. He explained that he urgently needed a birth certificate. It was not difficult to obtain a birth certificate. His name would be on one of the registers.

'Still, it's useful to have contacts these days,' repeated the bricklayer, in conclusion.

One confidence led to another, and more people contributed their grievances. The two latest arrivals also chipped in. The stockier of the two, who had come to fetch his son's birth certificate, argued that officials did not care and that they lacked a sense of duty towards the public. Then, when someone approached, they all stopped talking. The bricklayer shared out pieces of kola.

He got what he had come for. As he left, he shook hands all round. Then it was Dieng's turn.

'Man, let me breathe a little,' said the clerk, lighting a Camel. He began a conversation with a colleague at the other end of the office.

The hold-up continued. Behind Dieng, a woman's voice rose in protest:

'Stop grumbling,' snapped the clerk, returning to his seat, with bad grace. 'You! What do you want?' he asked Dieng in a sharp voice that stung his ears.

'Me?' said Dieng, his thoughts interrupted.

'It's your turn, isn't it? What do you want?'

Like an eel, a beggar in a lofty turban and carrying a long string of beads suddenly slipped between them. He intoned:

'Ngir Yallah, Dom. By the grace of God, son.'

'Clear off,' the official jumped down his throat, first in French, then in Wolof. 'Good God, you are here morning and afternoon, splitting our ear-drums.'

Sheepishly, the beggar withdrew.

'Well, you, what do you want?'

'Me? ... A birth certificate.'

'Where were you born, and what was the date?'

'Here are my papers.'

'I don't need your papers. Your date of birth, and the place?'

Put off by the harshness of the man's tone of voice, Dieng looked around him for support, a frightened expression on his face. He showed his papers again.

'I am waiting, man,' the clerk said again, puffing at his cigarette.

'Come on, hurry up,' complained the woman behind Dieng. 'Can't anyone help him?'

A man in a bush-jacket came up.

'Go back to your place,' ordered the clerk bossily in French.

'Come now, speak politely,' replied the man.

'What? Don't show off.'

'Please note that at least I am polite,' objected the man and, turning to Dieng, read aloud to the clerk from his papers:

'Ibrahima Dieng, born in Dakar about 1900,' stated the man

'The month, I need to know the month.'

'I tell you, about 1900.'

'And you think I am going to hunt for it? I am not an archivist.'

These exchanges took place in French. Little by little, they became more heated until a violent quarrel broke out between the two clerks and the public. Everyone was talking at once. The man in the bush-jacket held his ground. He vehemently reproached the young man for his lack of civic sense and professional conscience. He took Dieng as his witness, but Dieng said nothing. He kept out of it. Although he recognized the justice of the accusations levelled by the man in the bush-jacket, he could not see their usefulness. Things began to turn nasty, for the woman impudently attacked the mentality of the administration since Independence. She spoke loudly: for more than a week she had been coming, morning and afternoon, and if anyone thought she was going to pay a bribe or open her legs, he was mistaken. 'She has no shame,' thought Dieng. He did not have the courage to tell her to be quiet and wondered if someone else would.

At last, an orderly arrived and calmed the woman. This had its effect on everyone else and voices dropped.

'Your date of birth,' the clerk began again.

'Ibrahima Dieng, born in Dakar about 1900,' stated the man in the bush-jacket.

'How many months are there in the year?' asked the clerk, irony at the corners of his mouth.

'Twelve,' said the man, glaring at him.

'In which month was he born, then?'

'Listen, friend,' intervened the old orderly, addressing Dieng. 'Listen carefully. In your quarter there must be someone whose date of birth is the same as yours ...'

'It is written here,' said Dieng, bristling. 'I have my voter's card. The date is on it.'

'Excuse me,' said the old man, brushing aside the man in the bush-jacket who, raising his honest face to look at him, saw in the orderly's eyes that gleam of madness that is characteristic of the obstinate. The old man addressed Dieng, whose clothes had impressed him.

'You are being fooled with your voter's cards,' he said in French. 'No one is going to be bothered about voting. You see all those registers? Well, there are even more in the basement. Every one of them will have to be gone through, one by one.'

'Can't he leave his name on a piece of paper?' said the man in the bush-jacket, intervening again. 'Then someone could search for it.'

'Do you want to teach us our job? If we did what you say, he'd wait more than two months.'

'That beats all!'

'Do as he advises you. Find someone whose date of birth is the same as yours,' said the woman, making her contribution.

Dieng suppressed an inclination to tell her it was all her fault.

'Or else find someone with influence,' the old orderly whispered into Dieng's ear.

'Who can I go and see? The imam at the mosque? No. He doesn't know anyone. He says so often enough. In this country you get nowhere if you don't know anyone with influence. The proof! Since I've been out of work, I have been promised I'd be taken back. All the other men I worked with have been taken back,' he soliloquized. From the Place de l'Indépendance, he walked towards the Sandaga market.

At the crossroads, he looked around for someone he knew who would lend him twenty francs. All those closed faces were unknown to him. All those eyes, those mouths, those ears seemed to be without pity. Who could he go to? That man hurrying past? No, he could not behave like Gorgui Maïssa. A young man caught his eye. He reminded him of a distant cousin who lived nearby. The desire to go and see that distant cousin took shape in his mind. 'It would look as if I had come to sponge,' he said to himself. His hesitation was due to the fact that this distant cousin, who had recently come back from France, was married to a white woman. But the idea of going to see him persisted and finally got the upper hand. He would only ask him for twenty francs. He would not be able to refuse that.

He arrived in front of a wrought-iron gate. He examined the courtyard before deciding to place his finger on the bell. A cold sweat broke out all over him. A houseboy in a white apron came and let him in.

'Masser has just come home,' said the boy, taking Dieng into the sitting-room.

He was greatly impressed. The feeling that he was an intruder gnawed at his inside. His gaze went from one object to another.

Everything here imposed silence. He didn't dare sit down. He hoped he would only see his distant cousin, and not madame.

A man in shirt-sleeves of about thirty entered the sitting-room. As soon as he saw Dieng, he hastened to put the 'old man' at his ease, asking him for news of his family and their relatives. He called madame and his two children, to introduce them.

Madame did not remember this uncle. How could she put a name to all those faces she had seen just once, three years ago, and which had since disappeared from her horizon? Hadn't her husband said, during a conversation among mixed couples:

'Here, our relatives and in-laws only come to see us when they want something. So, why should we bother ourselves with African social custom?'

Dieng declined their invitation to stay for a meal. He had only called to find out how they were. When he left, the distant cousin went to the door with him. Alone with him, Dieng made his request. The cousin went back inside and returned with a hundred-franc note and a cheque for a thousand francs. He had no cash in the house. The uncle thanked him and promised to call on him again at his office the next morning.

Back in the sitting-room, the cousin found madame in a sulk:

'Money is all they ever think of, and that was all he wanted.'

He understood his wife's feelings, and looked at her with sympathy. The notion of the mutual responsibility that helps and sustains the members of the same community in time of need was foreign to their milieu.

'It is hard for us, but it is harder for them.'

Madame stalked out of the room.

Left alone, the distant cousin reflected: how was he to make his family understand they must only come and see him at his office?

———————

AT THE BUS CENTRE, DIENG CHANGED HIS NOTE. THIS would obviate the need to show a hundred-franc note and thus excite the envy of a relative encountered by chance, or oblige him to pay his fare. The bus was full. Next to him, on a bench for two, an old man with a worn, lined face was talking to a well-dressed man sitting opposite him.

'I didn't see the fellow you are talking about,' said the old man. in a Cayor accent.

'You did give it to him?' asked the other.

'He wants too much.'

'Everyone has his price. The main thing is to get what you want.'

'Where is the country going to? Every time you want something, you have to pay.'

'Speak softly,' advised the younger man, looking round at the other passengers.

Dieng had missed nothing of their conversation. He was sure the old man had just had to bribe someone to obtain a service. What? If only he knew. He watched them through his eye-lashes. The younger man inspired him with confidence because of his neat dress. He had the shiny forehead of a believer.

The driver's assistant collected the fares. Dieng gave him two ten-franc pieces.

At the Gumalo stop, the old man and his companion got off. Dieng did likewise and walked abreast of them for a while.

'Excuse me, brothers, I heard you talking just now.'

The younger man's face darkened with fear, and he mumbled: 'We said nothing, my father and I. You must be mistaken.'

'That's right, man, your ears have deceived you. It was some other people you heard in the bus,' the father put in.

'Don't worry, I am not what you think I am.' .

'Yallah is our witness that we said nothing. We are both Muslims. My father is from up-country. He came here to go to the hospital. That's all. We have paid our tax. Here, take this and buy yourself some kola.'

Dieng was flabbergasted. How can you make people believe you? The old man's son thrust a hundred-franc note into his hand. Before he even had time to draw breath or say anything, the father and son were at the end of the road. Dumbfounded, he stood there, holding the note with the tips of his fingers.

It was after two o'clock when he walked up the main street towards the bank. On the pavement, there was an unbroken flow of people, and a constant coming-and-going of traders selling sun-glasses, cuff-links, lengths of cloth, combs, tailored trousers, statuettes and masks; very young shoe-shine boys; women selling groundnuts and blind people: every hundred yards, a human milestone sat on the ground, chanting. Human trunks on wheels propelled themselves between the legs of the passers-by.

Outside the *Africa* bookshop, Dieng was accosted by a discreetly-dressed woman. She needed ten francs to return home to Yoff. She had been robbed of all her money. There was nothing in her tone of voice or in her behaviour to suggest she was a common prostitute. Dieng sympathized with her and gave her twenty-five francs, repeating to himself the ritual phrase: 'May all my misfortunes follow these twenty-five francs.'

'Perhaps I know her family. How thoughtless of me! I don't know her name, but I'm sure I'll recognize her again,' he said to himself as he continued on his way. She had thanked him, wishing him all possible happiness.

The bank was not open yet. The clerks were waiting outside the staff entrance. Looking at the various groups in turn, he sought a familiar face. Near a pillar, he noticed a stout man, dressed in a well-cut suit and carrying a large brief-case. He examined him at length. The man sensed that he was being watched. Then Dieng went over to him.

'If there is money here, there is nothing to fear, you will be paid,' was the reply to his question.

Another man approached. He was thin; his tweed jacket was too big for him and sagged at the shoulders. They spoke in French, which Dieng did not understand.

'Why didn't the person who gave you the cheque make it payable to the bearer?'

'What do you mean, the bearer?'

He did not get his explanation. He arranged with the man in the tweed jacket that he would present himself to him when the bank opened. In the meantime, he must go round to the other side of the building and enter by the public door. When it opened, a crowd streamed into the hall of the bank. Dieng went and sat down, his heart beating. From time to time, a mechanical, vibrant voice called a number, and a man or a woman went up to one of the windows.

A toubab came and sat opposite him. Fear seized his stomach. His eyes met the toubab's a third time. He saw the toubab's gaze linger on his face and on his trembling arms. A strange, indefinable feeling came over him, like a feeling of guilt. His fear gave him the impression he was committing some wrong. Instinctively, he recited the protective verses of the Koran.

The mechanical voice disgorged a number. The toubab got up. Dieng followed him with his eyes, and his breast heaved a long sigh of relief. A hand on his shoulder sent a shiver down his spine.

'Brother, you are wanted over there.'

Behind the counter, the man in the tweed jacket said to him, in a low voice:

'This is your number. Listen carefully for it: 41. Ask the cashier for hundred-franc notes.'

Dieng went back to his seat, repeating to himself: 41 ... 41. It was not long before it was his turn to present himself at the window. The cashier asked him how he wanted his thousand francs. As he was leaving the bank, the young man in the tweed jacket stopped him:

'Alhamdoulillah!' said Dieng. 'Everything went well. Thank you!'

'Uncle *(there were no ties of family between them)*, I beg you to think of my colleague. It is thanks to him that you have your money.'

'How much?' asked Dieng.

'You are a father of a family. Instead of four hundred francs, give him three hundred.'

Dieng thought the figure was rather high.

'Remember, my colleague was taking a risk. For your thousand francs, he risked his future and his family's welfare.'

Hearing him expatiate on the risks his colleague had taken, Dieng gave him the three hundred francs. He grumbled about people who expect to be paid for every little service they render. But he also had to acknowledge that without their help, people like him would find life difficult.

On his way back, with the money in his pocket, he looked in all the richly laden shop windows. Outside the *Service des Domaines*, a crowd attracted his attention. It was gathered round an old beggar who was holding forth. He had hollow, empty eyes, his cheeks were like a pair of horse's bars, and he had a strong, piercing voice. Dieng felt in his pockets.

'Father! ... Father! ... Please!' he heard a woman's voice say next to him. 'Father, forgive me, I am a stranger to Ndakaru. I came here to find treatment for my husband, and Yallah has called him to him. Now I must return to my village. I appeal to your generosity, to the grace of Yallah and his prophet Mohammed.'

There was nothing about her reedy voice, with its even tone, to inspire either pity or morbid condescension, only a shining lake of tears welling up over her eyelids.

Dieng stepped aside to the left to allow two men to pass.

'Voi! Voi!' he exclaimed. 'I saw you just now. I even gave you twenty-five francs. It was a little further on, over there.'

Dieng was convinced it was the same woman, the same eyes, the same elongated face. Only her clothes were different.

'Me?' she cried, her hand on her breast. 'Me? You must be mistaking me for another woman, man.'

'No! No! Yallah is my witness.'

People were beginning to look round at them with hostility.

'Go on your way, man! I am not what you think I am. I am an honest woman.'

'How was it, then, just now, on this very pavement ...?'

'Man, go on your way,' she interrupted him again. 'You look like a marabout, and I would never have believed this of a respectful man like you.'

Dieng spluttered:

'If I am to say nothing, you, too, should keep quiet.'

'I left a father like you at home. Dressed as you are, you ought to be ashamed to make propositions to the women you meet,' she concluded, moving away.

Disconcerted, Dieng looked around him. He heard people condemning him. The sweat of shame broke out on his forehead. A man of his age, in the white uniform of a chauffeur, took him gently by the arm and led him out of the crowd.

'If honest people take to begging, where will it all end?'

The chauffeur did not reply. A little further on, he left Dieng and went on his way.

There was no point in getting the bus. With the money he had left he would go to a photographer and buy a stamp. In the Avenue Blaise Diagne, he examined the photographers' windows. In one of the studios, a Syrian woman with a tired face, her head covered in a white veil, asked him in Wolof:

'What do you want, man? Have your picture taken?'

'I only want to find out how much an identity photo costs.'

Without getting up from her stool, the Syrian woman told him the price. He thought it was too high. Five or six others all quoted the same price. He would have liked to go to Salla Casset, who had the best reputation, but the price put him off. In the end, he went to Ambrose. A small fellow with a very funny walk, Ambrose met him at the door of his studio, a disused garage. He sat Dieng down without giving him time to draw breath even. His apprentice, familiar with his employer's technique, adjusted the two lamps. They were so bright they forced Dieng to shut his eyes.

'Don't close your eyes, man. Is it for an identity card? Good. I knew it was as soon as I saw you. Raise your chin. That's right! Ready. There, it's done.'

Dieng found himself on the other side of the curtain. Ambrose took two hundred francs from him, saying:

'Tomorrow.'

Late into the night, forgetting his unfortunate experiences, Dieng lay thinking happily of the days of security ahead. He congratulated himself on his great perseverance. He tossed and turned in his bed. He thought about the reply to Abdou he would dictate to the letter-writer. Suddenly he remembered the fifty francs. He dictated:

> *I have received your letter and money-order. For months we have been worried about your absence Everyone was anxious about you. One day, one of your friends told us: 'Abdou has gone to France.' What you have done is not good. How could you go away without telling us, especially me? You know me, you could have told me. Perhaps I would have opposed it; simply because I would have been afraid for you. But knowing you are a good son, you would have had my blessing, especially as you were going away to work. For here there is no work at all. I am happy, very happy, to hear that you have found work.*
>
> *So, you are in a foreign country. You are alone, without anyone to advise you. No one to tell you what you must and must not do. You are your own father and mother. Avoid bad company. Think, too, that you must come back. Your mother only has you for a son, and eight children to feed. Your needs must come after hers. Here life is getting more and more difficult.*
>
> *As soon as I received your money-order, I did what you asked. I sent three thousand francs to your mother. I expect to hear from her in a few days. Perhaps she will come herself.*

Dieng wondered whether he ought to mention the distant cousin. Better not to tell everything. He returned to the mental composition of his letter.

> *I am keeping twenty thousand francs for you, as you asked me to. I think you should send all your money to me. If you do that, I'll buy you a house for when you come back. Youth doesn't last forever.*

He had dictated enough. Aram, whose aiye it was, received him twice.

The next morning he went to the distant cousin's office. The latter drove him to the town hall in his mini. He told him to wait with the old orderly, who recognized him. They talked. The distant cousin eventually came out with someone else. 'He looks like a boss,' thought Dieng. He watched them from a distance, and was struck by their familiarity with one another. The distant cousin beckoned him with his finger. He wrote Ibrahima Dieng's date and place of birth on a piece of paper.

'Come back the day after tomorrow, uncle, and go up to the first floor,' the distant cousin's friend told him.

It was over. The distant cousin was unable to drive him all the way home, but dropped him at the Sandaga crossroads. As they separated, Dieng seized his hands and opened his palms, muttering verses from the Koran. The distant cousin let him have his way. Out of the corner of his eye, he saw a policeman approaching them, feeling his chest pocket. When he reached them, the policeman looked at the two pairs of hands, at the man's face, then at the marabout (for he thought Dieng was one), and he joined his hands to theirs. Dieng took hold of one of his thumbs. He raised his forehead and his lips moved. Two passers-by stopped and held out their hands. When he had finished murmuring, Dieng sprayed saliva all around. They all replied, 'Amine! Amine!' and rubbed their faces as they broke up.

Gaily, Dieng returned home. He thought how he would have his birth certificate the day after the next and his photo the next afternoon. He had forgotten about the stamp.

———

FOR THE REST OF THE DAY, HE HAD NOTHING TO DO. THE following day he had to go to a baptism and then to a funeral. He could not get out of it. After the ceremonies at the mosque, he made his visits to the relatives and friends. On the Saturday, for reasons that were not very clear, he decided not to go to the town hall, putting it off until Monday.

In the afternoon, he went to Ambrose the photographer. The shop was closed.

When he returned home, he found his elder sister, Abdou's mother, had arrived. She was a large woman, with broad hips. Her face had been deeply lined by the Cayor wind and the whites of her eyes had turned brown. When the greetings were over, in her rough, unemphatic voice, she explained the reasons for her visit. She wanted to leave again the next day. She had received her son's letter and had come to collect her three thousand francs. Dieng told her about his efforts to cash the money-order and that things looked hopeful. It was only a matter of days. Two, three at the most. He had even been to see the distant cousin, who had been very polite to him.

'Him! The son who now ignores us! And to think I used to wipe his bottom!'

'We have to understand …'

'Hasn't he deserted us? We who bore him, nursed him? Because he has become a toubab. Don't talk to me about him. He knows we are desperate. I still have my dignity. I shall leave here without going to see him.'

'And your husband?'

'In the bush. I'm alone with the children, and we have nothing. Nothing at all. I had to borrow from left and right to get here. Even these clothes I have on, some of them belong to my second veudieu,' she explained. Her anger was evident from the way she spoke.

Mety brought the brother and sister a meal. As they ate, she insisted Dieng must find at least two thousand francs, so that she could leave the next day.

'I have nothing to buy my return ticket,' she said in conclusion.

'The rice you are eating was advanced to me at a ruinous price. I have only two hundred francs left.'

'I have also contracted debts after receiving Abdou's letter. And I promised to pay them when I got back. How can I return empty-handed? It is unthinkable. Go and see your friends.'

'I'm afraid times are hard. Life isn't what it used to be. You can't count on your neighbours any more. Nowadays everyone looks after himself.'

Dieng did all he could to moderate his sister's entreaties. She launched into a bitter diatribe. She talked about life in the country, where two months of hard work were followed by one normal month, during which there was just enough to eat, and then three months of chronic famine and depopulation. Several times, Dieng tried to silence his sister. 'You should only say such things in a closed room to people you are sure of.' She spared nothing and no one. Raising her voice, she lamented that there were no brave men like there were in the past.

Aram came to her husband's aid. Tactfully, she invited her sister-in-law to rest after her tiring journey.

'I'll go and see what I can get,' said Dieng.

'Don't come back empty-handed,' she told him.

As he was leaving, Aram drew him aside and said:

'Try and sell these.'

It was a pair of gold earrings that Dieng had once given her.

'I'll find something without that. Keep them.'

'It is dark. If you find nothing, go to Mbarka. He doesn't turn his nose up at gold.'

Outside, he reflected. Who could he borrow two thousand francs from? No name or face came to mind. He knew from the outset that he did not have a hope. No one would help him. He was unlikely to find such a large sum of money in times like these, he concluded. He decided to take a long walk and then return home. Tomorrow, he would see. He knew his sister's obstinacy. She would spew out her anger, and that would be that.

From the shadow emerged the ghostly, shrivelled outline of Nogoi Binetu, draped in her cloth. She was accompanied by one of her grandsons, a nine-year-old lad. They recognized each other in the dark. She was on her way to Ibrahima's house, she said. (Contrary to custom, she only used the family name on ceremonial occasions.) She asked Ibrahima to sit down beside her on the bricks.

'I was on my way to your house to ask you to lend me some food or some money. I need fifty kilos of rice.'

Dieng had guessed the moment they had met. The old woman's voice wound its way slowly through his brain.

A hawker crossed the road, chanting:

> *Powder to kill fleas, bugs and cockroaches.*
> *Powder to give you a restful night.*

'I am on my way to Mbarka's. I'll call on you when I come

back,' murmured Dieng, thinking to himself: 'It's no use telling her I haven't anything.'

They parted.

Two broad rays of light from the shop projected themselves onto the sand. By a door on the right, three men were comfortably installed around a stove on which mint tea was brewing. They were the shopkeepers of the street. They were engaged in lively conversation.

Dieng greeted them and went into the shop, where Mbarka was serving a customer.

'I hear your sister has come. Did she have a good journey?' inquired the shopkeeper, by way of greeting.

'Alhamdoulillah!' acquiesced Dieng. 'May Yallah be thanked!'

'Amine! Amine!'

'You came in to greet me?' Mbarka went on, anxious to avoid mentioning Dieng's account in front of a witness. 'Choose a nut from the bottle. I have been expecting you for days.'

Dieng selected a firm nut, broke it and held out his hand, first to the shopkeeper, then to the customer. The aroma of mint filled the air.

'You have come, I hope, to settle with me,' began Mbarka when the customer had left. 'You know I never badger my customers.'

Dieng tried to plead his case, swearing by the name of Yallah. Now he had his sister on his hands. Finally, he showed Mbarka the earrings. The shopkeeper examined them with an air of disdain, and handed them back.

'Mbarka! Mbarka!' called a voice from outside.

'I'm coming,' Mbarka called back.

'I only want five thousand francs for them. I'm sure I will be able to cash the money-order on Monday. I will come and see you before anyone else, inchallah. Help me, in the name of Yallah and his prophet Mohammed.'

'Yallah! Yallah! Do you think I make five thousand francs in a day?'

With purposeful gestures, he leafed through a register with a greasy cover inscribed in Arabic lettering. His index finger ran down the page.

'There! ... Do you know how much you owe me?'

In a rapid, monotonous voice, he listed the various articles and concluded:

'You owe me twenty thousand seven hundred and fifty-three francs. And you have done for seven months.'

'Eye! Mbarka!' called the voice again.

'I'm coming,' he called back, still looking at Dieng.

The light from the ceiling made the top of his forehead gleam and the dark patch under his eyes extend down to his mouth, which jutted out like a dog's snout.

'Yallah knows I cannot. Go and see someone else and think about paying me, for I'm closing your account.'

'Listen,' begged Dieng.

Mbarka was already with the others, leaving him alone in the shop.

The shopkeepers sat around the stove, while one of them, his legs crossed, officiated: raising the teapot high, he poured the infusion into the glasses, where it landed with a dull sound, scenting the air.

Dieng stood watching them sip the hot drink greedily. His silhouette stood out against the pool of light.

> *Powder to kill fleas, bugs, lice and cockroaches.*
> *Powder to give you a restful night.*
> *Who wants some? It isn't expensive.*
> *Once I'm home, I don't go out again.*
> *And don't come and wake me, please.*
> *Please, I have a young wife. Come on!*
> *Buy some now!*
> *Powder ... Good powder!*

It was the hawker, who had stopped for a moment.

'What do you want, my friend?' one of the shopkeepers asked Dieng. He was reclining on the pavement, holding his foot, bent over, with his hand, so that it was off the ground. Speaking in their dialect, Mbarka put them in the picture.

'Let me see!'

Dieng leaned over to him.

'Are they gold?'

'Pure gold. Hallmark gold. I want to pawn them for five thousand francs. I paid eleven thousand five hundred francs for them.'

'I'll go and see.'

He got up and went into the shop. When he came back, he spoke to Mbarka. Then he addressed Dieng:

'We haven't any cash, as you know, but I see you really need money. I'll take them for three days.'

'Agreed.'

'Wait. I'll take them for two thousand francs. You will give me five hundred more.'

'Two,' countered Dieng, squatting down next to the man. 'I need five thousand francs, but give me three thousand. Mbarka knows I have a money-order from Paris.'

'I was trying to help you! Take back your jewelry. It isn't much use to me. It's tied money.'

The shopkeepers lost interest in him and returned to their conversation. The glasses passed from hand to hand. Dieng tried, but in vain, to invoke religious solidarity and the law that required each man to help his neighbour. Nothing made any difference. In the end, he accepted the two thousand francs.

'Listen carefully, my friend. If in three days—Monday, Tuesday, Wednesday—you don't come to redeem your earrings, you lose them and I will sell them.'

'Yes.'

'Think carefully.'

'I tell you, I have a money-order.'

The other man turned to Mbarka. They spoke in their dialect, which Dieng could not understand. Mbarka took the earrings, went into the shop, came back and counted four five-hundred franc notes into Dieng's hand.

At this moment, Gorgui Maïssa arrived. After exchanging greetings, he walked along with Dieng.

'Each time I call on you, Mety or Aram tells me you are out. I have just seen your sister. She has lost weight, poor woman.'

'I'm always on the go these days.'

'I see everything is in order.'

Dieng did not reply. He was calculating: five hundred francs for old Nogoi, the rest for his sister. He would have liked to refuse Nogoi her five hundred francs, but he could not. 'She must have a gree-gree to force my hand,' he said softly to himself.

'Will you lend me two thousand francs? I'll pay you back at the end of next week. I am also expecting some money,' said Gorgui Maïssa.

'Oh?' grunted Dieng, interrogatively, roused from his inner conflicts. 'I can't.'

'Try! Please, try! I'd be happy with even a thousand francs.'

'Maïssa, I cannot, believe me.'

'Ibrahima, people must help one another. Don't enjoy what you have by yourself. Think of others. Today it's you, tomorrow it will be someone else. Man's remedy is man.'

'Maïssa, the money you have just seen I obtained by pawning my wife's earrings. It is for my sister. I don't know myself what I am going to give my wives tomorrow for the day's expenses.'

'Still, you promised Nogoi something.'

'Ah!'

'I went to see her. She told me she was waiting for you.'

'I haven't cashed the money-order. Yallah is my witness. And the money-order isn't even mine.'

'I know,' replied Gorgui Maïssa, holding him by the wrist. 'You have known me for years. Think of the old days! We didn't hide anything from one another. As soon as I receive the money I'm expecting, I'll settle with you, down to the last sou. I'll even make it more. Help me. You know I don't want it to go on the spree. It's for my family ...'

'Maïssa, this money is not mine. This money-order that you are all building your hopes on is not mine.'

'I know. Before your nephew comes back from Tugel (Europe), I'll pay it back.'

'I haven't any money,' said Dieng sharply, going into Nogoi's house. 'It is a waste of time telling people the truth these days,' he thought.

Being hospitable sisters-in-law, the two wives did not allow Abdou's mother to leave empty-handed the next day. Each had taken from the bottom of her trunk a choice garment to give her as a present. Her brother took her to the bus station, promising to visit her within a week at the latest. She had a great deal to say, and never stopped nagging him about her problems.

'Instead of trying to raise yourself to a more respectable place in society, you just squat in filth,' she told him.

On the Monday morning, after leaving the town hall with his birth certificate in his pocket, Dieng went on to Ambrose, the photographer. Twice he found the garage door closed. No one could tell him why it was closed. Was the photographer sick?

A heavy weight fell from his shoulders when, in the afternoon, he saw from some way off that the door was wide open. The apprentice told him that the proprietor was out. He did not know when he would be back. Yes, he did recognize him. He was the bringer of bad luck! Their camera hadn't worked for two days!

'Give me my money back.'

'Pa! Wait until the boss gets back. All I know is that the photos are a failure.'

The apprentice, seated on the edge of the table, with his feet on the chair, was ogling the naked women in the pages of *La Vie Parisienne*. Dieng grew impatient and fidgety as the wait dragged on.

'When you know your camera doesn't work, the honest thing is to give the money back. Did I haggle over the price? No! ... If your boss doesn't give me the photos, then he must give me my money back.'

'Pa! It's not my business. Stop bawling and wait. You are frightening our customers away,' said the apprentice, without raising his eyes.

'I've got children! My youngest is older than you.'

The apprentice lit a cigarette, indifferent.

'I was told to come back last Friday. It is true what they say about the children nowadays. You aren't even born yet, and already you are smoking.'

'Pa! It's not your money.'

As he spoke, the apprentice blew the smoke in Dieng's direction. He could not stand the smell, and the smoke went down to his lungs. It made him choke, and he coughed, clutching his throat. His cap fell off. Angrily, he tried to grab the adolescent.

'Pa! Careful now! I'll hurt you,' said the apprentice. 'Pa! Take care,' he said, pulling the table and turning it over. 'Look what you have done, you old fool.'

'Me? Wait till I get hold of you, you'll see!'

In a flash, the adolescent dealt Dieng two or three rapid blows on his nose with his fist. The blood spurted out, all over his clothes. The noise had attracted the passers-by, who collected outside the door.

'This Pa didn't find my boss in, so he wants to break the place up,' explained the apprentice, held now by a man from the crowd.

'You have no right to break a workman's tools. His boss is out, so you wait,' was the opinion of the man who had come between the two antagonists.

Wiping the lower part of his blood-covered face, Dieng had difficulty in putting across his own version of events.

'You are wrong,' the man said with severity. 'You don't fight in someone else's workshop. What can you do with these marabouts! They're a bunch of frauds.'

'Kebe, what's happening,' inquired a young woman with a strong Ndar-ndar accent, pushing her way through the circle of curious bystanders. Her headscarf made her look like an Amazon. Kebe, the pompous fellow, turned round:

'Nothing, Bougouma. It's this fake marabout who's been given a hiding by Malic.'

'Laihi lâh!' exclaimed Bougouma, the young woman, holding her chin with her hand in her surprise. 'He's swimming in blood,' she said. 'A real battering-ram. So, it's the fashion, now, in Ambrose's shop.'

'Come, man. I live next door. I'll give you some water,' put in another, older woman, with a look of pity.

As he followed her, Dieng explained all the ins and outs of his misadventure.

Dieng had cleaned himself up and was sitting on the work-bench in front of the woman's house. He was watching the photographer's studio. After an hour, he saw the little man approaching gaily in the distance, greeting all he met. He was on his home ground.

'So, there you are, you old Jonah,' he said in French when he caught sight of Dieng.

When he saw his studio, his happy expression froze into a hard mask. Erupting like a volcano, he broke into one of those rages to which Malic, his apprentice, had never accustomed himself. A tornado of curses battered Dieng's pious mind.

'Boss, he's the one. I swear it was he,' said Malic.

Dieng had seen people angry before, but the photographer belonged to an unusual category. His neck and face swelled up. His dark black skin turned a pale grey, his eyes stood out and rolled, bloodshot, and his lower lip dropped and twisted itself, showing his teeth discoloured by the cheap wine sold in all the bars of the Medina.

'Boss, I told him to wait, but he wouldn't listen. Look what he did,' added Malic, throwing oil on the fire.

Ambrose fulminated against all the Diengs in the country. His angry, aggressive voice attracted the attention of the passers-by:

'Get out! Get out, before I do something terrible. Do you think your miserable two hundred francs will pay for all this damage? Idiot! Stupid fool!'

Ambrose let him have it in every language. His great consumption of detective novels, his assiduous frequentation of cinemas where the cheapest kinds of French, American, English, Indian and Arab films were shown, had ripened his vocabulary.

Dieng was crushed, stupefied. His first impulse had been to

answer back, but he had been put off by the photographer's sudden attack. He said nothing and, like the curious bystanders, he listened to the other man's tirade.

'Old man, go,' advised someone in the crowd.

'He owes me money,' retorted Dieng, seeking, with his eyes, the support of a man of mature age wearing a caftan in a shade of egg-yolk and a chocolate-coloured arakiya on his head. Still looking at the man, Dieng continued:

'Days ago, I ordered some identity photos. Now, he and his apprentice refuse to give them to me. So let him give me my money back.'

'Ambrose is a crook. In spite of all the scandal he causes, the police never trouble him,' contributed someone in the crowd.

Ambrose leapt forward, snorting like a piglet.

'Who said that? Who is the son of a whore who said that? Let him show himself. The damage this old fool has done will cost me thirty thousand francs! Look at the mess! I am going to the police about it.'

Dieng turned a watery gaze on the photographer, then towards the man in the arakiya:

'There is no law in this country. You owe me money and you talk,' objected Dieng, in a moment of lucidity.

'Man, I implore you, go, quickly.' It was the man in the arakiya. His eyes met Dieng's. He repeated, in the same calm voice: 'I advise you to go.'

Somewhere, Dieng felt a pang. The blood flowing warm through him, making his heart ache, warned him of danger. Had he said too much?

'An informer,' murmured someone in the crowd, which suddenly melted away in fear.

'He owes me money,' Dieng tried to say again, raising his worried brow to the man in the arakiya.

'Where are you going?' the latter asked him, firm.

Dieng felt bewildered. A vague, lethargic heaviness held him rooted to the spot. In an instant, this feeling left him, and the effort restored his energy. His tongue was paralyzed. But the fear of imminent humiliation strengthened the concern for his pride that came over him, and helped him to make up his mind to leave, to escape before the crowd surrounded him again. Speaking in the voice of a child, he said to the man in the arakiya:

'This way.'

The man ordered him to go with a nod of his head. A hundred yards on, Dieng looked back. The man was standing like a statue, watching him.

We must try and understand Ibrahima Dieng. Conditioned by years of blind, unconscious submissiveness, he fled from anything likely to cause him trouble, be it physical or moral. The blow of the fist he had received on his nose was an *atte Yallah:* the will of God. The money he had lost, too, it was ordained that it was not he who should spend it. If dishonesty seemed to have the upper hand, this was because the times were like that, not because Yallah wanted it so. These were times that refused to conform to the old tradition. In order to rid himself of his feeling of humiliation, Ibrahima Dieng invoked Yallah's omnipotence: for he was also a refuge, this Yallah. In the depths of his despair, and of the humiliation to which he had been subjected, the strength of his faith sustained him, releasing a subterranean stream of hope, but this stream also revealed vast areas of doubt. He did not, however, doubt the certainty that tomorrow would be better than today. Alas! Ibrahima Dieng did not know who would be the architect of this better tomorrow, this better tomorrow which he did not doubt.

———

DIENG DID NOT WANT HIS NEIGHBOURS TO SEE THE STATE he was in: his clothes spattered with blood, and his babouches as well. He had a precise notion of the esteem which he had come to enjoy since the advent of the money-order. For a week he had been on his own, and on his own he must face adversity. After he left the main street, he kept close to the fences, hurrying, unhappy but stoical, from corner to corner, his head low, and reached home without being seen by anyone.

He entered his house.

Aram leapt up to meet him, her eyes bright with fear. She looked at their husband's face, and down to his babouches. Dieng met her battery of questions with silence. Anxiety spread its dark carpet over the woman's heart.

In the room, Dieng lay down. With each heartbeat, his groans grew louder. Blood began to pour from his nose again. Her arms on her head, Aram let out another long, plaintive cry.

'Don't, it is nothing,' said Dieng, dabbing his face with a cloth.

'What happened to you?'

'Nothing. Stop bellowing. You'll bring all the neighbours out.'

'Lahila! he is dead,' she cried, at the sight of the blood, and rushed outside, her arms on her head.

In the yard, her cries grew louder, and the neighbours came running and assailed her with questions.

'He is inside, dying,' she wailed. 'His blood is flowing like the water at the fountain.'

Old Nogoi, still active in spite of being so skinny, marched into the room, followed by Mety. Disgruntled faces waited. For several days the Dieng family had been watched; everyone, deep down, wished them ill, without admitting it to themselves.

'He is going to die,' whimpered Aram again.

'They tried to kill him! As soon as he cashed the money-order, three men threw themselves on him,' Mety hastily declared in a loud voice. Making the most of the general consternation and the surprise effect of her announcement, she went on, in a plaintive voice, her eyes brimming with tears:

'If the money had been his, Yallah knows, we would not suffer so much. It was his nephew's money, who works in Paris. His sister came to fetch her share, and it is only thanks to Aram's earrings, pawned to Mbarka, that she was able to go home again. Now we have lost everything. Everything, even the esteem we had in the quarter because of the money-order.'

For a moment, everyone responded to the feeling of solidarity that binds the needy.

'Don't cry, Aram, and you, too, Mety,' said one woman.

'Everyone thinks we are selfish, that we are trying to get out of our duty to our neighbours.'

'Mety, don't heap us with shame! You hurt us. True, we heard of the money-order. What do you expect? When you are all one family and you are hungry, you believe what you hear. You know that people blame before they will understand.'

'It's because we are hungry,' another woman added. She had bulging eyes, like pearls, and was wearing an old, faded dress.

Tongues loosened, and the most secret thoughts emerged into the light of day: intrigue, nepotism, unemployment, immorality, the indifference of the authorities. Voices grew loud, and outstretched arms gesticulated wildly into the empty air. The amount of money involved came under discussion.

'A hundred thousand francs, stolen in a single day!'

'I'd heard he had been given a year's back-pay. He hasn't had work for more than a year.'

'His nephew is coming from Paris by aeroplane.'

'Let us hope and pray to Yallah that this nephew is a good Muslim and will forgive him.'

The collective monologue then returned to the state of the country: corruption, debauchery, police informers.

Old Nogoi re-appeared.

'Alhamdoulillah! He's asleep. Losing so much blood at his age! What sort of a country is this? I no longer count my years and I have never left Ndakaru, but I confess I do not recognise this country.'

More than an hour later, as evening fell, the women withdrew. The house was quiet. A small fire glowed sadly in the kitchen.

During the two days that Dieng kept to his room, he had plenty of leisure to reflect and to think about the money-order, to approach modern life analytically. Whenever he pushed his mental investigations too far, everything became blurred, and he lost himself in his head, as the local saying goes. It was a vicious circle. He felt suffocated. People seemed to be becoming more and more evil, with no respect for the property of others. As the old adage said:

it is easy for the enterprising to live off the careless.

The men of his age-group came in after prayers for a chat. They all seemed to believe Mety's story. After they left, he reflected moodily about his first wife's allegations. What was he to do? He would have to start the process again, find at least three hundred francs for the photos and fifty for the stamp. After all he had spent, he could not afford to let the money-order be sent back. There were still four or five days to go before the fateful date.

It was the end of the morning, and he had worked out a careful plan. The children were playing, as usual, in the road. He scolded Mety severely, but she replied:

'Now you are in peace. You can come and go without having to say: 'Yallah is my witness, I haven't cashed the money-order.' You wasted your time invoking Yallah and swearing by his name and the name of his prophet Mohammed, no one believed you. It was being said everywhere that you had received a year's salary in back-pay. Others were saying your nephew had sent you two hundred thousand francs to build yourself a house. No one would speak to us, your wives. At the public fountain, they all came to us: 'Advance me a kilo of rice', 'Lend me a hundred francs', and so on. It was unbearable to have to say the same thing always. Tell them the truth? They wouldn't believe it. It's simple: the truth isn't any use any more!' said Mety.

'You must always speak the truth. However hard it is, you must always speak the truth. Now what am I going to say? You know very well that the money-order is still at the post-office.'

'So, you can go about cashing it without having people spying on you. People come specially to see what is cooking in our pots, so that they can say afterwards: "There, they have had the money." No, it isn't lying. It is simply a case of forestalling the unkind thoughts they have about you. And remember, Aram lent you her earrings for your sister. And the day to redeem them has passed.'

'I know that. You don't need to remind me, nor to insinuate that I prefer my sister to my wives.'

'Ibrahima, forgive me,' began Aram. 'We'll forget the earrings. If Yallah wills it, as soon as you are better-off, you can buy me some more. Possessions don't save us from death, but from dishonour, for your possessions are ours. Mety is right. Forgive me for contradicting you. It was impossible for either of us to cope with all the requests. According to the gossip of the neighbourhood, we were selfish. All their hunger was channelled and directed at us.'

'Living with neighbours who are your enemies is unbearable. And you know yourself that we aren't the only ones to falsify the truth. We hide ourselves from one another. Why? ... No one has enough for his family to live decently. This new behaviour is the result of our wickedness. Life isn't what it was during our youth, during the youth of those who are the parents of today. How many people hide their bag of rice at night? And why? So as not to share.'

'What am I going to say when it is known that the money-order is still at the post-office?'

Mety raised her forehead. Her headscarf, tied on one side, emphasized the shudder that shook the lower part of her face. In her eyes was the light of accusation, which said: 'Is he really a fool, or does he think we are?'

'When the day comes, say it was Mety who lied.'

'Me, too,' said Aram.

Dieng retreated before their determination. 'I will have to lie to the end,' he thought.

Still weak and hollow cheeked, he walked like a convalescent. Outside the entrance, he inspected both sides of the road, and then made his way to the corner where Mbarka's shop was.

'Ibrahima ... Dieng,' announced Gorgui Maïssa by way of greeting. 'And your health?'

'Alhamdoulillah!'

Maïssa, his brow furrowed, watched Dieng suspiciously. Dressed in an ample indigo blue boubou, Dieng, with a deft, habitual gesture, gathered it behind his back with his hands.

'You were very ill the other day ... Where did it happen? ... It is hardly credible.'

'I have difficulty myself believing it. Yet ... Well, honesty is a crime nowadays in this country.'

'Ah!' exclaimed Gorgui Maissa, his mouth open, revealing the stumps of his teeth discoloured by kola juice. The brightness of the sun surrounded his irises with faint specks of silver, and a network of folds fanned out across his rough skin. Sceptical, he said:

'Perhaps you are right. But why do you say it? Is it right to plant different kinds of seeds all in the same field?'

'If the field is worthless, it doesn't much matter if the different kinds of seeds are all planted in it.'

'The complete possession of an object gives power to its owner. And impartial owners are rare.'

'A little knowledge in a variety of subjects, however little it may be, makes any fool wise in the midst of fools. I said and I say again that honesty is a crime nowadays in this country.'

Having said this, in order to escape from Maïssa, he went into Mbarka's shop.

Mbarka was serving two women. With a note of deference in his voice, he returned the new arrival's greetings.

'In spite of that cursed debt, I would have come to see you. Perhaps Aram did not pass on to you my greetings?'

'Oh, yes, this very morning.'

'It is unbelievable! What will become of us if it goes on like this, having one's wallet stolen in broad daylight! Have you been to the police? It is their job to catch robbers.'

One of the women, Daba—'the black-one', was her nickname in the quarter—turned her coarse, voluminous face towards Dieng as she counted her tins of milk.

'You are right. I was thinking of doing it this morning,' said Dieng.

'You should have done it straight away. People will begin to doubt,' said Mbarka. Then, addressing Daba: 'Judging by the way you treat them, you'd think these notes had no value.'

'If you don't want them, I'll keep them. I'm not a miser.'

'Daba, you are the tip of a spear! Whatever you touch and whatever touches you, it's always the same, you draw blood.'

'Why do you turn your nose up at these notes? Isn't it enough that you cheat people? Do you want us to go down on our knees as well?'

'What are we going to do, Ibrahima,' asked Mbarka, changing the subject. 'My friend, you know these goods don't come from our country. I have my own commitments. The people I owe money to are not like me. They only know dates. Make an effort. While I think of it, it is too late now to redeem the jewelry you pawned.'

'I have only one word,' said Dieng, leaning on the counter and wondering what he would say to Aram about her earrings.

'I have a message for you.'

Mbarka came near and leaned over to Dieng, with his mouth against his ear. Slowly Dieng's face darkened and his features hardened.

'Never!' he suddenly exclaimed. 'Never! Sell my house? Why? To pay you? Is that what you want? Tell whoever it was sent the message that Ibrahima Dieng will not sell his house. Never! Poor, that's bearable, but poor with no house, that's death.'

'Don't shout.'

'You have the cheek to ...'

'And the money you owe me? I couldn't care less about your house. You owe me money. Pay it. That's all! For I, too, can shout. All your fine clothes are just wind. Yesterday, when you grovelled for a handful of rice, you didn't shout so much.'

'You gave me credit because I pay. Everyone knows you charge more than you should.'

A crowd gathered, invading the shop.

'You can die of hunger, you and all your family. No more credit for anyone. By my ancestors, you will pay me. I will go to the police.'

'Come, then! Come on!' yelled Dieng, grabbing him by the wrist.

'Let me go! ... Let me go, I say.'

'Come on!'

'You'll pay me, I swear it. But I'll never give anyone credit again.'

'Mbarka, address your remarks to Ibrahima Dieng,' intervened Ibou. 'And you, Dieng, remember, he who owes money should be conciliatory.'

'Ibou, I've had enough of being conciliatory. I'm not a mattress. Speak for yourself. Would you sell your house? Answer me!'

'It was a message, that's all! You owe me money and you shout louder than I do. You say you were attacked! You're bluffing. You want to profit from your money-order on your own. But you will pay me.'

At this, Dieng felt adversity weaken and give way. He straightened up, morally sure of himself. His eyes met others in which shone the light of accusing doubt.

'I was with him, Mbarka. Don't breathe poison into people's hearts,' declared Gorgui Maïssa, who had approached, his eyes on Dieng's bent brow.

'I doubt all the same. And you'll pay me before you leave the shop.'

Don't say that, Mbarka!'

'Leave him. Everyone knows he had dealings with shady characters.'

'That is my business. No more credit for anyone.'

'Our husbands pay. Mine paid you yesterday,' objected one woman.

'It's true. When you owe money, you must pay it. The debtor must be careful of the language he uses to his creditor.'

'You, Daba, you have always been friendly with this robber Mbarka,' Mety intervened, roughly. A little girl had fetched her from the public fountain.

'I wasn't talking to you, Mety.'

'And I, Daba, am talking to you,' countered Mety, facing her. Mety's quarrelsomeness was legendary, in spite of her age. After Daba, she turned on the shopkeeper.

'What we owe you I have in my head. You will be paid. But we won't take ourselves to pieces to sell our flesh.'

'I am not talking to you, Mety. This is an affair between men. I am talking to your husband. He owes me money, and his name is in my register, there ...'

'Quite so. It's because it's my husband, and I was the one who bought the things. You have added it up and so have I. If it's

because of the money-order, you will have to swallow your saliva.
He has been robbed.'

She gesticulated vehemently, shaking her index finger in Mbarka's face.

More and more people gathered:

'Money! It's crazy how people fight over money since independence,' said a man in babouches, making his way through the
crowd with his shoulders so as to have a better view.

'A curse on the man who invented money,' agreed a woman next
to him.

'It is true. Money seems to have taken the place of morality in
our country,' said someone else at the back.

'Yet all we want is enough to live on and to enable our families
to live.'

Suddenly, a burst of laughter rocked the crowd:

'Shit!' exclaimed Mety in French, for the third time.

Old Baïdy, all skin and bones, made a dramatic appearance.
Tall and thin, his gaze swept the crowd. A few days before, when he
had returned home empty-handed after his visit to Dieng, he had
said to his wives:

'I'd rather die with hunger in the belly than hold out a hand to
the Dieng family.'

Pompously, he declared:

'Truth for truth. When you owe money, you pay.'

'The man who has donkeys must be on the side of the owner of
the hay. There is no virtue in paying your debts when you are rich,'
Mety retorted, refusing to be quiet, in spite of the pleas of her
husband and other people.

'When a man surrenders his authority, he becomes a scarecrow,'
objected Baïdy, his eyes riveted on Dieng.

'A man is only a scarecrow when he is nothing but words. There
are men and men,' declared Mety, with energy.

The old man withdrew.

The women backed Mety, and formed a group round her.
They called the shopkeeper all the names they could lay their
tongues to.

Mbaye's black 403 drew up at the other door. With a lithe, feline tread, he entered the shop. His European clothes and his reputation in the quarter gave him a certain authority. He spoke gravely to the assembled people and within fifteen minutes had restored calm. The crowd dispersed. Walking away with Dieng, Mbaye asked:

'Uncle Dieng, I waited for you this morning.'

'I meant to come and see you, but then I fell into this ...'

'It's over now!' Mbaye said, interrupting him. 'Come and see me at two o'clock.'

He climbed into his car and the engine roared. Gorgui Maïssa came and sat beside Dieng as the car drove away.

'He's somebody, Mbaye,' he declared.

'Thank you for just now in the shop.'

'It's nothing. We must stand by one another whatever happens. A tongue hurts more than a bullet.'

The 403 turned at the first intersection.

Mbaye belonged to the 'New Africa' generation, as it was called in some circles; men who combined Cartesian logic with the influence of Islam and the atrophied energy of the Negro. He was a businessman, always ready to do a deal, asking a percentage on each commission according to its value. It was said of him that there was no difficulty he could not resolve. With a villa on the far side of the southern sector, he also had two wives, one a Christian and the other a Muslim, and a 403. He had reached the top.

Mbaye's villa stood in the middle of the shanty town and its tumbledown shacks. In the sitting-room, crammed with armchairs, chairs and vases of artificial flowers, blue was the dominant colour. Theresa, the Christian wife, who was on the point of leaving for work, received Dieng and installed him in the sitting-room. She wore a floral dress and a Brigitte Bardot wig.

'Mbaye is having his siesta,' she told him in French, in her thin, reedy voice.

Seeing that Dieng was perspiring, she turned the electric fan on. Dieng looked around enviously at the furniture, and thought:

'Here is a man who has made it. Abdou will be like him when he returns from Paris.'

More than ten minutes passed before Mbaye entered the sitting-room, knotting his tie.

'What! You should have woken me to say there was someone,' Mbaye said to Theresa, who was impatiently glancing at the door.

'You said nothing to me, my friend,' she replied, still in French.

With a younger man's deference to an older man, Mbaye made his excuses.

'It is nothing. I came a little early. I understand. You must be tired.'

Taking care not to exaggerate too much, Mbaye spoke at length about the terrible disadvantages of modern life. He did not even have time these days for his siesta. According to his doctor, he ought to go to France for a rest cure.

A maid came in with a tray of coffee.

'Bring another cup for uncle.'

'No, thank you, I don't drink coffee.'

A car hooted three times. Theresa immediately rose, saying:

'Don't forget to turn the fan off ... See you this evening.'

'Remember to phone that man. Tell him I'll go to Rufisque this afternoon.'

'Okay.'

'Eskeiye!' exclaimed Dieng.

'Our country is making progress. The women have the same rights as the men.'

Saying this, he sipped his coffee. Dieng told him all about his recent difficulties, and even about the false story put out by Mety.

'Women are sometimes geniuses. I think it was a good idea. We'll go to the police station. First, we must get power-of-attorney. You will make me your proxy. For we haven't any more time to waste on an identity card. At the police station, there won't be any problem. You will have your money-order the day after tomorrow at the latest.'

'Inchallah! I am in your hands.'

'Oh!' said Mbaye, suddenly modest. 'There is a good chance

that the money-order hasn't been returned to your nephew yet.'

He finished his coffee and turned the fan off. His first wife appeared. She was in African dress. The introductions over, she took her husband aside.

Outside, Dieng was overjoyed. He did not know yet how much Mbaye would want. He did not know himself how much he would give him. A thousand francs? It was very little for a man like Mbaye. Five thousand? That was a lot. Two, three, four thousand? He would see.

They collected the power-of-attorney form at the post-office and then Mbaye drove to the police station. All the way, he did not stop giving Dieng advice for his nephew, Abdou. Sitting next to him, Dieng nodded agreement. As Mbaye had led him to expect, everything went smoothly at the police station. The power-of-attorney form completed, it was soon made legal.

'Uncle, it's finished now. I am a little late for an appointment at Rufisque. I'll be back this evening. Tomorrow morning, I shall go to the post-office myself.'

'Inchallah!' said Dieng.

'Inchallah!' echoed Mbaye. 'Come to my house at midday tomorrow.'

'Inchallah! I shall be there. Without you, I don't know what would have become of me.'

'It's nothing, uncle. We must help one another. Here, take a taxi. I haven't time to drive you home.'

'No! No!' Dieng tried to refuse the five-hundred franc note Mbaye held out to him. 'I can get back on foot.'

'Take it, all the same.'

Dieng could not get over it. Tomorrow he would have the money-order. With the five hundred francs in his pocket, he decided to go and see the letter-writer.

The bus dropped him outside the post-office. It was half empty. The old letter-writer only had one customer in front of him. He did not recognize Dieng. Dieng reminded him of the fifty francs and settled his debt. The letter-writer adjusted his glasses and took up his ball-point pen:

Dakar.
19 August 196 ...

Dear Nephew,

I am writing to ask you your news and to give you news of the family, which is excellent. Thanks be to Yallah! All of us here are thinking of you and pray to Yallah for you.

At last, I have the money-order. I didn't have an identity card when it arrived. Thanks be to Yallah, all is going well. Your mother came. She is well. Now she has gone back again. She only stayed one night, because of the work in the fields. I gave her her three thousand francs. She thanks you, greets you and prays for you. She asks you to send her some money to buy clothes and to pay the tax. This year all the prices have gone up. Last year's harvest was not a good one for them. You are her only support in the world.

For my part, I pray all the time for you. As soon as I received the money-order, I did as you asked in your letter. If it pleases God, you will find all your money here, even if Yallah calls me to him. I thank you for thinking of me and for having confidence in me. Nowadays it is so hard to have confidence in people. I beg you not to regard money as the essence of life. If you do, it will only lead you onto a false path where, sooner or later, you will be alone. Money gives no security. On the contrary, it destroys all that is human in us. I cannot tell you everything that passes through my head,

The letter-writer stopped. He raised his eyebrows above the metal frame of his spectacles. His customer seemed to be dictating his letter with a lump in his throat. Over the edge of his eyelids tears ran down in a clear stream. Dieng raised his head. Indeed, he, a grown man, was crying.

'Forgive me, man. It is my nephew. He is in Paris and he behaved like ...'

'Here I see and hear all kinds of dramas.'

'I was saying only this morning that honesty was a crime in this country.'

'I am listening,' said the letter-writer, catching sight of another customer waiting. 'You had got as far as: *I cannot tell you everything that passes through my head.*'

I thank you again. I'll never forget your confidence in me. Your aunts Mety and Aram and all the family greet you. With my next letter. I'll send you some gree-grees. Even though you are not in Ndakaru, you must protect yourself. Someone could put an evil spell on you. There is a real marabout here. I'll go and see him for you. I am very pleased to hear that you do your five prayers every day. You must go on doing them. Do not forget that you are a foreigner in Paris. Here, all the boys of your age have villas.

I have no more to say to you. You are a man.

Your uncle,
IBRAHIMA DIENG.

'The address?' asked the letter-writer, after reading him the letter and sealing it.

Dieng felt in his pockets.

'I have left it at home.'

'Never mind. You can find someone to write the address for you.'

In the street, Dieng, his heart beating for joy, generously gave ten francs to an old leper.

At home, he magnanimously forgave Mety the outrageous words she had used to the old man Baïdy.

'I understand why you did it. Our honour had been offended and in public.'

Afterwards, he went to join his peers at the mosque. There, before witnesses, he apologized to Baïdy, who said he felt no malice.

'Still, I want to know that you forgive me. And my family, too,' repeated Dieng, drunk with satisfaction.

'I tell you, I forgive you.'

'Alhamdoulillah! May Yallah forgive us. Me, too, I forgive you.'

'Amine! Amine!' said the onlookers.

'This is what we mean by being Muslims. To be simple and open towards one's neighbour. May Yallah keep us on that path.'

Gorgui Maïssa, whose mind was greatly exercised by Dieng's verbal exuberance, remained wary, watching him out of the corner of his eye.

When the gewe was over, Dieng replied evasively to his questions. So, late into the evening, Maïssa kept a watch on Dieng's house: who knew, but he had the money-order and would have rice brought into his house when night fell. They were long, uncomfortable hours of vain waiting.

The next day, excited by the feverish euphoria of the humble in their hopefulness, Dieng made a tour of the neighbourhood, conscious of himself as a man who belonged to a community. Everyone sympathized with him over his unfortunate experience, and offered him words of consolation. He repeated each time:

'A man needs enough to feed his family. When everyone has enough to eat, there will be peace in men's hearts, everywhere.'

Several times he put his hand in his pocket and felt the letter intended for Abdou with his fingers. It was crumpled. He thought: 'Mbaye will give me another envelope.'

Back home, he called out:

'Mety, have you seen Abdou's letter?'

'No. Perhaps Aram has.'

'Me? I haven't seen it either. Look among your papers.'

'You can never find anything in this house. Yet I certainly left it here,' he grumbled at everyone.

He found it in one of his pockets.

When the tisbar prayer was over, he went to Mbaye's house.

'Hullo, uncle,' Theresa greeted him. 'My man is out.'

'Didn't he leave a message for me?'

'Yes, he did,' she replied, patting a rebellious curl in her wig into place. She went on:

'I was waiting for the car, to drop it at your house. There is a sack of rice for you. It was delivered at midday.'

'I think there is a mistake,' he said, after a long pause.

'No, no, uncle. I haven't made a mistake. Mbaye left me a note. That damned chauffeur is never on time. Let's go inside.'

'When will he be back?' asked Dieng, sitting in the same place he had occupied the previous day.

'Uncle, he said nothing. He has gone to Kaolack.'

'Perhaps he will be back this evening?'

'I don't know, uncle. All the same, I'll go and ask my veudieu.'

She came back a moment later.

'She knows nothing either.'

'I will call again,' said Dieng, getting up, with the heavy weight of disappointment on his shoulders.

'You won't take the rice, uncle?'

'I'll wait for him to get back.'

Outside, his thoughts were in confusion. Until late into the night, he went back and forth between his house and Mbaye's. Each time, his anger grew along with his disappointment. At home, neither of his wives asked any questions. Everything about his manner gave away his anger.

The next morning, he went to say his beads in front of the villa. Towards eight o'clock, at the same time as the maid, he entered the sitting-room. The first wife, her forehead marked by a ring of sand (she had just finished her early morning prayer), asked him to wait. In less than half an hour, Mbaye came out, dressed, with his briefcase in his hand.

'They said you had been yesterday. I am sorry, I was at Kaolack yesterday.'

'I know you are busy,' said Dieng.

Mbaye's presence had given him renewed confidence, and his optimism returned. All the angry reflections of the night before burst like soap bubbles.

'You didn't take the sack of rice,' Mbaye began.

He was interrupted by the arrival of the maid to serve breakfast.

'Be quick,' he said to her. 'Bring the butter in the paper; the butter in the dish is off. Uncle, you'll have some coffee?'

'No, thank you.'

'With milk,' insisted Mbaye.

'No, thank you. I prefer my quinqueliba.'

'I have the coffee bug. To be brief, I don't know how to tell you. You are my uncle. About the rice. I was calling on my Syrian, and since he had some rice, I bought some for you. I was thinking of the disagreement you had with Mbarka.'

'I don't know why it was.'

'Anyway, you did right. I couldn't explain it all to the women. You know what they are like.'

Mbaye spoke carefully, to make sure he was understood.

'I did in fact cash the money-order yesterday. I had some business in Kaolack, which I had to see to in person. When I got there, I parked my car opposite the market. You know Kaolack? A town of crooks! Leaving the car, I crossed the market. I bought something or other, and when I came to pay for it, I felt for my wallet. It had gone! Not only were your twenty-five thousand francs in it, but sixty others as well.'

'But ...,' Dieng began. He was unable to continue.

Mbaye dipped his bread in his coffee. Dieng lost nothing of the gymnastics of his jaws.

'It's like I told you.'

Their eyes met.

'You don't seem to believe me, uncle. Still, I am telling you the truth, the absolute truth. I swear it by the name of Yallah. At the end of the month, I will pay you back. I am the victim of my kindness.'

'No, no, my son. I am the father of a family. For a year now I have been out of work. Besides, that money isn't mine.'

'You think I have cheated you? No! Mety is a relation, and that is why I wanted to help you.'

Dumbfounded, Dieng found it hard to react, even morally, as he usually did. He opened and shut his hands mechanically. He could find nothing to say.

'Listen, uncle, here is my wallet and the five thousand francs I have. I give them to you. Take them. Yes, I know the money-order isn't yours. I'll have the sack of rice taken round to you. If I did not know you, I would say you did not believe in Yallah. At the end of the month, I'll bring you the balance. If, in the meantime, you need anything at all, don't hesitate to come and see ͬ .'

Mbaye called the maid and said:

'Have the sack of rice in the next room put into the car. Come, uncle.'

Dieng was shattered. Anger and disappointment deprived him of all will to act. The violent reversal of his hope seemed to have destroyed his brain. Whatever it was, he followed Mbaye out. He saw two men take the sack.

He said, stating a fact:

'It's not a hundred-kilo sack, it's fifty kilos.'

'Yes,' replied Mbaye, interrupting him and tapping him on the shoulder. 'It was all I could get.'

The 403 dropped him in front of his house. With Mbaye's help, he unloaded the sack. Before he drove off, Mbaye made him a firm promise.

The fifty-kilo sack of rice lay outside the door. The passing housewives cast greedy eyes in its direction. One, plucking up courage, went up to Dieng.

'Is that rice, Ibrahima?'

'Yes,' he replied.

'Really, rice? If only I could have some!'

'You would like some?'

'Yes, Dieng.'

'Put down your calebash.'

He filled it for her. The others also presented their containers. Without a word, Dieng proceeded to distribute the rice. In less than thirty seconds, perhaps a minute, the news had spread.

'Ibrahima Dieng is giving away rice.'

Mety and Aram came running. They pushed the outstretched arms roughly away.

'Are you ill, Ibrahima?' remonstrated Mety.

'I was.'

Somehow the two wives managed to drag the sack away, as the other women hurled insults at them.

'Go back to your homes. It is finished,' said Aram, coming back to fetch their husband, who had remained outside.

'I am not mad!'

'Ibrahima, why this foolish prodigality? Where have you ever seen, since the world began, the poor throwing away rice? Even the rich don't do it. And you ...'

'And you, what?' interrupted Dieng, sitting with his head between his hands. 'It's your Mbaye ...'

'Mbaye Ndiaye?'

'Yes, Mbaye Ndiaye! I gave him power-of-attorney and he has stolen the money-order. Instead, he has given me a half a sack of rice and five thousand francs.'

'What? The money-order?'

'And my jewelry?'

'Àram, always selfish! Stop thinking of yourself. Do you know how much I have lost on account of that money-order?'

'And what about all that I have borrowed!'

'All that you have borrowed, Mety?' asked Dieng, looking up at his wife.

'The fifteen kilos of rice were used up long ago.'

'The money-order was not mine.'

'People of the house, are you in peace?'

'Peace, only, Bah!'

The postman sorted through the bundle of letters in his hand.

'Ibrahima Dieng, what is going on? In the next street, I heard you were giving away rice.'

Dieng told him. Bah lifted the visor of his cap and declared:

'What you did was an act of despair.'

'It's over now. Me, too, I am going to put on the skin of the hyena.'

'Why?'

'Why? Because it is only cheating and lies that are true. Honesty is a crime nowadays.

Bah handed him a letter, saying:

'It is from Paris. It has the post-mark. You think everyone is corrupt? No. Not even those who have work are happy. Things will change.'

'Who will change them? I have been out of work for a year because I went on strike. I have two wives and nine children. Only cheating pays.'

'Tomorrow, we will change all that.'

'Who is 'we'?'

'You.'

'Me?'

'Yes, you, Ibrahima Dieng.'

'Me?'

A woman entered, a baby on her back, and interrupted Dieng with her greetings.

'Master of this house, by the grace of Yallah, I implore you to help me. For three days my children and I have only had one meal a day. Their father has been out of work for five years. They told me in the street you were kind and generous.'

Dieng straightened up. His eyes met Bah's. The begging woman looked at the two men.

No one said a word.

GLOSSARY

adda   the tradition, customary law

aiye   the period during which the wife of a polygamous husband takes her turn to sleep in his hut

alcati   policeman

alhamdoulillah   May Allah be thanked!

allahou ackbar   God is most great!

arakiya   cap

babouche   slipper

barahlu   the eighth month in the Wolof calendar

beintan   the cotton tree

bilal   muezzin

boubou   voluminous dress worn by Muslims

chechia   military cap

diambur-diambur   a freeborn person

eiye   exclamation of surprise

el hadj   a Muslim who has been to Mecca

eskeiye   exclamation of surprise

eye   exclamation of surprise, or to attract attention; hey!

fadyar   the Muslim dawn prayer

garde-cercle   a rural policeman

gewe   religious service

griot   a member of the low caste of praise singers

guelewar   noble; a person of noble descent

gueweloi-diudu   a griot attached to a family to sing its praises and recite its genealogy.

inchallah   God willing!

kada   a kind of acacia tree

loli   the fourth season in the Wolof calendar

malaika   angels

marabout   a holy man

mbagne-gathie   bamboo screen

Medina   a populous suburb of Dakar

navet   the rainy season

navetanekat   a migrant farmer who hires himself out during the rainy season

nawle   social rank or class

Ndakaru   Dakar

ndiatigui   master

ndjiolor   noon

nebedaye   a dish made of edible leaves

nere   a tree

niaye   sandy flats of Senegal

nidiaye   dear

node   Muslim call to prayer

nyebe   beans

peinthiu   the village square

quinqueliba   a drink made from a plant with medicinal properties, especially against fever

rhun   a kind of palm tree

rysala   the five ritual prayers of the Muslim day

sahhe   granary; the hut for storing grain

samara   leather sandal

santa   family name

sariya   'the way', the Muslim code of law

sump   a thorn tree

sura   the chapters of the Koran

tacousan   the Muslim afternoon prayer

thorone   the first season in the Wolof calendar

timis   the Muslim sunset prayer

tirailleur   a soldier of the regiment known as the *Tirailleurs Sènègalais* (Senegalese Rifles)

tisbar   the last prayer of the Muslim day, said at nightfall

toubab   European

vehi-ciosane   white genesis

veudieu   co-wife

vradj   a thorn bush

yoryor   the Muslim noon prayer

yothe   draughts, played with pieces of stick and donkey droppings for counters

yothekat   draughts players